W9-AZG-967

DISCARD

"*Purgatory Road* is a taut and twisted race into the human heart; an absorbing meditation on surviving the wilderness around us, as well as the wilderness within. Only after turning the final page was I able to catch my breath."

—Josh James Riebock, bestselling author
of *Heroes and Monsters* and *My Generation*

"Samuel Parker brings a unique voice to fiction that is, at once, engaging and unsettling. His ability to breathe life and realism into even the most minor characters is one of the many reasons that *Purgatory Road* is an exceptional read. This book is definitely worthy of a big-screen adaptation."

—Booker T. Mattison, filmmaker, author, professor

PURGATORY ROAD

PURGATORY
ROAD

SAMUEL PARKER

Revell

a division of Baker Publishing Group
Grand Rapids, Michigan

© 2016 by Samuel Parker

Published by Revell
a division of Baker Publishing Group
P.O. Box 6287, Grand Rapids, MI 49516-6287
www.revellbooks.com

Printed in the United States of America

Library of Congress Cataloging-in-Publication Data
Names: Parker, Samuel, 1974– author.
Title: Purgatory road : a novel / Samuel Parker.
Description: Grand Rapids, MI : Revell, a division of Baker Publishing Group, 2017.
Identifiers: LCCN 2016029230 | ISBN 9780800727338 (pbk.) | ISBN 9780800728618
    (casebound)
Subjects: LCSH: Married people—Fiction. | Hermits—Fiction. | Suffering—Fiction.
    | Mojave Desert—Fiction. | GSAFD: Mystery fiction. | Christian fiction.
Classification: LCC PS3616.A7464 P87 2017 | DDC 813/.6—dc23
LC record available at https://lccn.loc.gov/2016029230

16   17   18   19   20   21   22   7   6   5   4   3   2   1

For Liz

PROLOGUE

The eighteen-wheeler pulled into the truck stop off I-15 and applied the airbrakes. The passenger door swung open and a young girl jumped out, waved a thank-you to the driver, and walked toward Las Vegas. She had a small backpack thrown over one shoulder of her denim jacket. All she had.

The driver had been a nice enough guy. He had picked her up along a stretch in Utah and enjoyed the company. He said that he had a daughter back in Memphis and that he couldn't imagine seeing her walk the roads out west at her age. When they pulled into Vegas, he handed her forty dollars from his beat-up wallet.

"Here, take it."

"You don't have to."

"No arguing now, hear?"

They both knew that she needed it more than he did. No doubt he also thought the money would soothe his conscience for leaving such a naïve creature on the doorstep of Sin City.

She walked most of the afternoon through the boarded-up streets northeast of the strip, thumbing the buttonholes on the jacket she held and wiping the sweat from her brow. The desert sun turning her shoulders red. She met the few catcalls and periodic requests for spare change with downcast eyes and silence. She was scared. This was not what she had come out west for.

Night crept in and the sidewalk shadows grew more menacing. She stepped into a party store and grabbed a can of Coke and a stick of beef jerky. She waited in line behind a fidgety man undecided on the best choice of liquor under five dollars, which he then paid for with two crumpled bills and a small mountain of change pulled from his sagging pants. Under the white light of the store awning, she sat on the sidewalk and ate her dinner.

The girl checked in to a rundown '50s motel that was half vacant. She did not want to sleep outside tonight. Not here.

"You eighteen?" the desk clerk asked as he wiped some crumbs off his stained wifebeater T-shirt.

"Yes," she replied without eye contact.

"Uh-huh."

He slid the key to her and snatched up the twenty-dollar bill she laid on the counter. She went to room 7. Lucky number, she thought.

She took a shower and pulled out a shirt from her backpack. It was dirty, but still cleaner than the one she wore on the way in. She would have to find a laundromat, but the thought of spending money from her dwindling supply on clean clothes seemed like an extravagance that she could not afford.

The girl dried her hair as best she could with her towel, curled up on the bed, and fell asleep.

She was awakened the next day by a pounding on the door. How long had she slept? She looked at the clock—half past noon. The pounding continued.

"You dead in there? You only paid for one night! You get out now!"

She ran around the room collecting her things and hustled out the door.

"You need another night?"

"No, I don't have the money."

"I'm sure we could work something out," he said, looking her up and down. Her heart rose to her throat and the combination of fear and loathing almost made her vomit. She turned and walked out to the street as fast as she could.

She wandered around aimlessly—mouse in a constantly changing maze. She saw the faces of happy tourists on the strip, enthralled with 100 megawatts of burning filament, and wished she could have someone to smile with.

She kept walking.

The girl's stomach roared, so she found a diner and stepped inside. She walked to a booth and sat down, grabbing a laminated menu. A middle-aged woman approached, sporting a classic "Mel's Diner" uniform, and looked her over.

"My, my, you look like you've been through some things," the waitress said, tapping her pad of paper. "What can I get you?"

"Some toast . . . and some water."

"You need more than that, honey. I'll get you something good."

Within minutes the girl was staring down a hot-turkey sandwich drenched in gravy and a side of potatoes. Thanksgiving dinner on a greasy spoon. She scarfed it down quickly as if someone would steal it before she was done.

"How much will that be?"

"Don't worry, honey, I got it. You want anything else?"

"Coke?"

"Sure thing."

The girl sat in the booth, drumming her fingers and sipping her soda while lost in a daydream, the bent end of the straw suffering from her half-conscious chewing.

She paid little attention to the people coming and going from the diner, and did not notice the man who sat down at the table next to her, nor did she seem to notice his constant staring. He ordered his food and began to eat but kept his eyes on her.

Coming to, she glanced over at him. "Can I help you with something?" she barked sarcastically.

"Naw, don't think so. Just wondering what runaway story you got."

"I'm not a runaway."

"Uh-huh. You planned on moving to the streets of Vegas?"

"I'm on my way to LA. Just passing through."

"How you getting there? You walking?"

She ignored him and looked out the window. The girl thought the conversation had ended until he sat down in the booth across from her. He brought his plate with him and kept on eating.

"You need a ride somewhere?"

"No," she shot back and got up to leave.

He grabbed her wrist and she sat back down hard. Fear coursed through her veins as she stared at the man across from her. His dark-sepia eyes were motionless, resting in their sunken sockets.

"Listen, missy. I ain't done nothing for you to be rude. I'm just trying to help. This city can get pretty mean. The bus station is way across town. It's a long walk."

His tone was soothing but firm. She thought about the fix she was in. Running low on money and coming from the motel with the repugnant clerk had put her on edge. Perhaps she was over-reacting. Maybe this guy just wanted to help.

The trucker from Utah was like that, but his Santa Claus appearance squashed any reservation she had had. The man across the table confused her. He was dirty, some might say greasy, but he appeared to be genuinely concerned.

Her shoulders eased. "All right, I'm sorry."

"That's okay. Now, Helen here can vouch for me," he said, pointing to the waitress behind the counter who continued on with her work, not noticing the conversation between her two customers. "She knows I ain't no crazy man. I just don't want to get home tonight and see your face on TV."

"All right."

"You got a name?"

"Molly."

"Molly?"

"Yes."

He scooped another forkful of food into his mouth and chewed, nodding slowly.

"Nice name," he said with a full mouth.

She watched him eat, studying his face as one studies the brush-strokes on a painting. Back home, the girl thought she was a great discerner of people. She would be at the mall with her girlfriends and would come up with backstories for the hapless shopper who crossed her gaze: that one is a trophy wife, that one is a banker but secretly spends all his money on porn, that one hates his life. But since coming out west, her powers had become unreliable. There was the clerk in Iowa who'd stolen her change, saying that she only gave him a five when she knew she had handed him a ten. There was the bus driver in Denver who wouldn't open the door until he got a good look at her backside. There was the guy from the motel who still sent a chill down her spine in retrospect. Now here sat a black-haired mechanic-looking local—another stranger she could not peg.

As he continued eating, she watched his hand move with the fork from the plate to his mouth and back again. She could see in the webbing of his hand, between his thumb and index finger, a blob of ink. Probably a tattoo poorly done. It captured her gaze as she tried to make out what the image was. He stopped eating and put his hand on the table palm down.

"Looks ridiculous, doesn't it?"

"What?" she said coming out of her daze.

"This tat?"

"I hadn't noticed."

"Uh-huh. Supposed to be a spider. Word to the wise, Molly, don't let some half-blind and half-crazy old man pin you down and ink you. It never comes out good."

She gave a small laugh and he smiled, exposing teeth weathered by the Pall Malls in his shirt pocket. Her defenses were slowly lowering as the man finished his food. He seemed all right, in that hick hillbilly way.

"How much money you got?"

"A bit."

"Probably not enough, huh? Let's get over to the bus station and see how much it is to LA." He stood up and walked to the door. "Come on now, the invite doesn't last all day."

Trepidation still lingered inside her.

She looked at the waitress, who was talking with another customer across the diner. She felt a pull to go to her, to look to her for guidance.

Molly thought about the woman back home who was probably sitting in her daughter's room right this minute, crying over her vagabond child. No, she could not go home now. It would smother her. She looked up at the man and decided, no matter how reckless, the only way was forward.

She got out of the booth and followed him outside. He opened the passenger door of an old black pickup truck and helped her get in. He slammed the door. The bench seat was stiff.

Molly eyed the man as he walked around the front of the truck, looking for the telltale signs of a sexual criminal or molester, as if the traits would be sewn into the fabric of his clothes, into the substance of himself.

He got in and fired up the truck. "Okay, let's get you taken care of."

PART ONE

THE HIGHWAY

1

They drove out of Las Vegas in the rental car, ready to explore.

Three days on the strip had gotten to both of them, and they were looking for a bit of breathing room. Too many lights, too many people. Neither of them were "Vegas" people, but it seemed like a cheap vacation spot away from the hurried Chicago hustle.

Overstimulus comes in different trappings, however; screaming city blocks have nothing on screaming one-arm bandits played by old blue hairs plopping down Uncle Sam's dime on the prospect of winning a retirement fund.

They had spent the previous night watching an ex–Navy chief in a scooter shooting craps, betting 6–8 in honor of his old aircraft carrier and absorbing drinks in sync with each losing bet. The crowd howled when he was busted and then tried, to no effect, to bet his scooter. He drove off, strains of laughter and some sympathetic eyes flowing behind him.

Yes, three days was more than enough.

They decided on no particular destination and just drove, letting the morning sun clear the cobwebs and smoke haze, enjoying the exchange of slot machine bells and dealer calls for desert wind.

They drove a blue convertible because he had decided on it. The Mustang with the black ragtop was not him on a regular day, but he was not playing normal life. He wanted to be cool, to be the guy who would buy American muscle and push it around every street corner. She went along with him, not fighting his childish urge to be hip for a day. She was good that way, he thought. She let him dream.

Grabbing the keys from the rental clerk, he had half skipped up the stairs and into the parking garage, looking for space 51. She followed meekly behind, watching him. He had opened the door for her, chivalrous out of character. He got in, tucked the Starbucks in the cup holder, fired up all the horses, and revved the engine like Vin Diesel. Yes, so different than the Volvo sedan he commuted in back home. Today, he would be fast and furious.

Cruising south down the strip, he was disappointed at the lack of a crowd to watch him drive. The zombie walk of a Vegas morning was all that greeted them. At each stoplight he would gas the engine a little bit more than needed, and she would roll her eyes and laugh.

The dream was skewered by the yellow Lamborghini that passed them going the other way. He was sure that was not a rental. He didn't rev the engine anymore.

They got off the main highway and drove west out into the desert. The two-lane meandered into the distance, so different from the concrete jungle they saw every day back home. The valley was circled by mountains, and from this vantage point they could still see Vegas some thirty miles away. It seemed so small, a speck on the horizon, where tens of thousands of people were doing things that people do when no one is watching.

The desert wind blew across the road, throwing dust on the windshield and cutting the shine on the hood. The couple could not think of another place on earth where the wind blew heat.

"I need to stop," Laura said.

"All right," Jack said, looking out the windshield at the rock and dust and sky. "You want to go right here?"

"No, just the next place you see."

They drove on for a couple more minutes and came to a small

gas station outside the city of Goodwell, population 127. It was a small single-pump station with a tiny convenience store attached. Jack pulled alongside the shack and parked the car next to a dusty black pickup, the only vehicle in the place. Laura jumped out of the car and darted for the bathroom door on the side of the building. *It's a good thing she doesn't complain about much*, he thought.

Jack walked into the store and headed to the vintage cooler in the back. The placed smelled like a combination of stale smoke and cat urine. The heat was somewhat lessened by a small oscillating fan screwed to the paneling over the door. How could someone pull a 9-to-5 here? Nothing like dreaming big.

He searched for caffeine energy drinks, but settled on four waters off the near-empty rack, and walked up the aisle toward the counter, his sandals sliding with the sand on the concrete floor. He picked up a bag of chips that appeared to have been made in the '70s. They didn't look too healthy, but there was nothing else to choose from.

Behind the counter sat a man with greasy black hair sticking out from under an old trucker cap. He was flipping through a magazine, a stream of smoke clouding his face from the overflowing ashtray next to him.

He was punk scrawny and wore an old blue mechanics shirt with the name *Colten* stitched on the front pocket. He did not look up as Jack placed his supplies on the counter and reached for his wallet.

Taking a slow drag off a nonfiltered cigarette, the man blew smoke across the counter, and it hung in the air thick like a London fog. "You getting gas?"

"No, just this."

"That'll be five bucks then."

"You take a debit?" Jack asked, putting his card on the counter.

"You getting gas?" The man lifted his eyes and pinned Jack with a dull stare.

"Uh, no . . . just this. Like I said."

"Cash only, Jack."

Jack stared back, trying to cover his shock.

"Your name's on your card."

"Oh."

"Spook easily, don't you?"

Jack put the card back in his wallet and pulled out a five-dollar bill. Colten took the money, opened the till, dropped it in, and slammed the drawer, all while staring Jack in the eye. He took another toke. His hands were rough-hewn out of burnt leather, tipped with dirty fingernails. *The hands of a mechanic*, Jack thought, *or a thug.*

He had seen guys like this when he and his wife would waste away a Sunday afternoon watching a *COPS* marathon on cable. Laughing at trailer trash, an American pastime.

"You sure that's all you need?"

"What?"

"Are you sure . . . that's all you need?"

"Yes."

Silence filled the room as Jack waited, wondering if the man was going to bag his things. The smell of fresh nicotine combining with the stale, musty air of the shop was suffocating, overpowering. He felt uncomfortable, worried, as if he had walked up on a rattlesnake.

"Is there anything else down this road?"

"I thought you had all you needed."

"Well, is there?"

"What are you looking for, Jack?"

"N-n-nothing, just w-wondered if . . ." Jack trailed off. He hated it when he stammered. Not since grade school had it been a real problem, when the school bully called his number on random days for his annual beating. He felt eight years old again.

"Wondered what? You want to see poor folk and misery? Is that fun for you?"

"No, it's not." Jack quickly became aware of himself—his overpriced, casual chic attire, the nouveau bohemian getting smacked with impoverishment.

The front door opened and Laura stepped up to his side, surveying what he was buying. Colten's face brightened as he looked at the new arrival.

"Howdy, miss. Beautiful day, ain't it?"

"Yes, it is," she replied with a smile.

Colten bagged up the goods, then pushed them across the counter, where Jack had to catch them before they went spilling on the floor. He stared back at the man, sensing the swarthiness flowing off of him.

"You folks out exploring?" Colten said, ignoring the answers Jack had provided.

"Yes," Laura started, "we just want to get away from the strip for a day. You know, see some of the country and all."

"Good a place as any to see it. We got a little bit of everything out here." Colten lifted off his hat and smoothed back his black hair. Jack expected to see Colten's palm covered in grease and sweat. The way the clerk smiled at Laura left him uneasy, nervous. The awkward silence of a stalled conversation filled the room, and Jack grabbed Laura's elbow and began ushering her to the door.

"That ain't your car out there, is it, Jack?"

Jack froze for a minute, and then turned back. "No, it's a rental."

"Thought so. You just like pretending for a bit, huh? Good place to do it. This country lets you be John Wayne for a day if you got the money. Is that what you're doing, Jack? Being John Wayne?" Colten's black eyes looked Jack up and down as if examining his soul through his skin. He squinted as he took another drag of his smoke, exhaling it into the empty shop.

"What do you know of it?" Jack lashed back.

A look of horror flashed across Laura's face.

"I know a bit. See it every once in a while." Colten waved his hand, shooing the smoke from the ashtray away from his face. "You two be careful now, the desert can be strange at times. Wouldn't want any trouble to come to you good city folk."

The silence returned, Jack and Colten locking eyes like two roosters in a pecking contest.

"We'll be fine. Thanks."

Outside the store, Jack pushed Laura to the car, and both got in. He was sweating and his heart was racing. His mind was trying to convince him that he was keeping himself from jumping the counter and punching the stranger, but deep down inside he knew it was fear.

Intimidation.

He hated that. He hated being intimidated. He hated it worse that he had allowed himself to be.

"What was that all about?" Laura asked, visibly upset at her husband's behavior.

"Just some local redneck trying to be tough."

"I thought he was just being polite."

"Yeah, I bet."

"What?"

"Nothing."

"Are you sure you're not the one with the problem?"

Jack stared back at her, ready to unleash the anger that he was too scared to let loose on Colten, but he checked himself. Why ruin the trip. Laura looked at him but didn't push it. He started the car and they headed west in silence along the two-lane road toward the mountains.

Intimidated. The word swirled through Jack's mind as they drove. He hated the feeling. He hated feeling immobilized by the posture of other people. From as far back as he could remember, he felt that way. Growing up, Jack admired the kids who would react, take charge, grasp the stick they were being beaten with, and turn the tables.

He thought about a little kid he knew in grade school named Dylan.

Dylan was a small kid but had the courage of a lion. There was one time on the recess yard when an older kid pushed Dylan down during a kickball game. Dylan got up, and even though he was only half his size, he pounced on the bully and bloodied his lip. When he was taken to the principal's office, rumor had it that Dylan told the principal to do his job properly so he wouldn't have to do it for him.

Adults don't really take to kids talking like this, and Dylan was rewarded with a three-day suspension. When he came back to school, he was a minor celebrity, one that Jack's mother said he couldn't hang out with anymore.

Jack's thoughts drifted back to the gas station. He worked up the script in his mind and mulled it over and over again, trying to get the scene with the most dramatic flair.

23

Take 1. Action.

Jack walks up to the counter and puts his supplies down.

"You getting gas?"

"Does it look like I'm getting gas, you white trash piece of . . . ,"
he would say as he reached over, grabbed the back of Colten's head,
and slammed it down on the counter. "Now bag this up before I
get angry."

Jack smiled. That would have been good.

Take 2. Rolling.

Laura walks in from the restroom.

"Howdy, miss. Beautiful day, ain't it?" Colten would say.

"You talking to her? Keep your eyes off her, you white trash . . ."
and again with the head slam to the counter.

Meanwhile, Laura had turned in her seat and was looking at
him. "What are you thinking about over there?"

"Nothing," he said, wiping the grin off his face.

"Uh-huh."

"Just thinking is all."

"Well, talk to me."

"All right, what do you want to talk about?"

"I don't know."

The silence returned.

And with that, Jack went back to working out the scenes in his
head. Always back to the head slam to the counter. Yes, the head
slam would definitely be the way to go.

Colten looked out the window of the convenience store and watched the blue Mustang spit rock as it roared away. He felt nothing. No seething hatred, no delayed viciousness. He just wished Jack to die.

Simple. Without thinking.

"You really are a piece of work," said the man at the counter. Seth.

He was dressed in a black button-down shirt with pearl buttons, tucked into vintage western jeans. An ornate silver buckle attached just below his abs. Seth looked the part of the evil cowboy in a Sergio Leone film, minus the hat. He was grizzled from the sun, lean and mean. Black hair greased back, much like Colten's, his pale white scalp peeking just past the hairline.

"Huh?"

"Just sayin'."

"Guy like that, car like that . . . due a beatdown if ever I saw one," Colten said.

"You can't tear 'em all down."

"Wish I could."

"Just your part."

"All right."

"Forget him. You got other things to think about."

Colten turned, grabbed the butt from the ashtray, took a long hard toke, and blew the smoke through the man. "Don't you worry, I got things taken care of."

Seth seemed unfazed by the toxic smog surrounding him. He could see fresh scratch marks on Cole's neck as he turned. "She do that to you?" he asked with a half smirk.

Cole brought his hand up and massaged the wound. "Let's just say this one's got a little bit of fire in her."

"Really?"

"Like I said, I got it taken care of."

"You got things taken care of? Ha! What do you know about getting things taken care of?" Seth said.

"I know enough. Got her locked up there right now."

Seth fingered the trinkets hanging from a spinner rack on the counter.

"Why do you do this? Play around? Should have been over and done with. Moving on to the next one. There are always plenty more coming each day."

Another slow drag, the amber glow lighting Colten's pupils. "This one's too good to rush through. I want to enjoy it."

"Always the same with y'all. Not able to see the forest through the trees." Seth stepped to the door but did not go out. He seemed to soak in the outside air by sucking in a deep breath. "Chaos, Cole. That's what you're working for. Don't get hung up on this girl and forget yourself. Nothing compares to that last moment, when they realize that it's over. That there's no going home. That there's nothing past that moment for them. You can string it along, thinking that you're having fun, but each second that goes by, you're leaving the door open for them. You do that, you're liable to get yourself in a tough spot. You're liable to mess it all up."

Another drag, another exhale. "Don't lecture me, old man," Colten said. "I've done this plenty of times."

Seth laughed to himself as he ran his hand through his hair. "All right, it's your show. Just remember this: every second is a loose end. You keep horsing around, others might want to jump in, change your plans."

"What do you mean?"

"Just sayin'. Keeping her out there like that, you never know who might be watching."

Colten extinguished the cig in the tray, reached down below the counter to grab a new pack, and was about to reply, but the man was gone.

4

After a while Jack and Laura managed to start chatting again. They made small talk as they admired the amazing views that they could not see at home: the valley floor butting up against mountain walls; the streaks of reds and tans that told the history of the world. The sun was in its full glory and the heat began to abuse the ground. They listened to the radio, Jack singing out the grunge hits from his high school days while Laura tried unsuccessfully to retune the dial. They finally settled on a classic rock station, and though the singer crooned about how sweet Alabama was, they took it as a fact that he had never come out west.

Slowly the station turned to static until it was completely gone, forcing them to shut it off. They were on the moon, gently riding the road as it coasted over rolling hills of rock and sand.

"We are in the boondocks now, huh?" Laura said.

"Yup."

"You think this is a good idea? We haven't seen another car for about half an hour."

"We're fine. We picked up some snacks and water, and we got our cells."

"I know, but . . ."

Jack grabbed her hand, which felt cool in the AC breeze. "Just a bit more. I want to see what's past that hill."

That had always been Jack's reason for everything. Never content with the present, he was always working for something beyond reach—one more degree, one more promotion, one bigger raise. One more hill. He explained it away as simple curiosity. She thought it was greed laced with ego. Always proving he was better.

Ambition is truly blind. It leads to no end, only constant searching.

Laura always went along with it. Even though the same mountains and valley peeked at them after each rise and fall, she held her tongue and let him do what he always did.

Laura was everything Jack was not. It was the only way they could get along. She was not the high school cheerleader, nor was she the valedictorian. Laura just was. She was the woman you pass on the street, admiring her good looks as she walked by, then forgetting she was there after just a few steps. She blended into her surroundings, unnoticed. Too often she went unnoticed by Jack, but she trudged on, silently carrying her loneliness and taking what scraps he offered her.

Twenty minutes down the road the car's dash began to flicker and the engine began to hiccup.

"Well, that doesn't sound good." Jack eased off the gas and coasted to the side of the road. When the car settled into the gravel, the power went out.

"Uh . . . dear?"

Jack knew that tone. It was the *I will appear patient, but you better get this fixed right now or you will suffer* tone. He turned the key in the ignition but got no response. All the electrical was out, and the engine would not turn over.

The silence in the car was amplified by the absolute nothingness of the desert.

"Maybe it just got overheated. Let me take a look."

Jack popped the hood and got out. He was slapped by the hot air as he opened his door, the radiation from the asphalt shooting through the soles of his sandals.

He gazed at the engine, but didn't know what he was looking for to begin with. He hoped that just by the sheer strength of his stare he could will the car back to life. After masquerading for a couple of minutes, he got back in the car and tried the starter again. Nothing.

"All right," he said, "let me call a tow."

Jack pulled his iPhone out and looked at the screen. No power.

"Well, that's weird. I charged this thing last night."

Laura grabbed her cell from her purse. Same issue. "Uh . . . dear?"

Again with that same tone. Jack's mind started racing for solutions. They were stuck in the middle of nowhere with not another soul in sight. The last sign of civilization was the town of Goodwell, and that had been a couple hours ago.

He decided to walk back up the road to the top of the hill. Before opening the door, he reached into the bag on the floor and grabbed two of the waters, handing one to Laura.

"I'm going to walk back there a little ways, see if I can see anything. You stay here."

She didn't argue with him.

Jack walked up the slow grade almost a half mile behind the car as the heat from the blacktop made his feet sweat and warmed his calves.

He looked back now and then at the car parked on the side of the road. With each step it appeared more and more insignificant in the great landscape around him. A small bit of metallic blue reflecting, shimmering like a watch in a sunbeam's path.

"Well, Jack, what are you going to do about this?" he said to himself. "It's hot, nobody around. Not good. Should have just stayed at the hotel."

When he finally crested the small hill, he had chugged almost his whole bottle of water and felt dizzy. After catching his breath, he stared out into a sandy sea of nothingness. Rolling rocks and blue, cloudless sky was all that caught his vision. He hoped for the subtle reflection of a car, or a tin roof trailer nestled among the cactus, but all he saw was desert.

The road they had come in on ran away from him into oblivion. Turning 360, the view did not change at all. They were stuck with no chance of help but what might come driving down the two-lane. He pulled the phone from his pocket again. The touchscreen was still unresponsive.

His mind began to race. An empty road could bring anything.

Jack envisioned a painted Indian in a dune buggy, wielding a sawed-off shotgun, bounding over the distant ridge followed by a stampede of Thunderdomers searching for fuel and slaves. Only problem was, he wasn't Mad Max and he knew it.

Or worse, he thought of a dusty black pickup cresting a distant butte and driving full force toward him. Colten, the hick gas pumper, exacting back-country vengeance on a city boy and stealing his girl. That was more of a reality, and it sent a pang of fear through his chest. He could practically hear the banjos playing in symphony through the mountain peaks behind him.

He shook off the visions. This wasn't a movie. This was real life, this was *what did I do to us* reality.

He stared back at the rental car, wondering what he was going to say to Laura when he got back. What could he say to his wife after he had driven them into an oven and slammed the door? He thought himself lucky that it was a half mile walk to the car. At the least, he tried to appreciate the absence of sound on his way back.

Loneliness is the acute sensation of realizing that you are on no-body's mind.

Of being the unneeded X factored out of all equations.

Laura stared out the windshield. The road ran off out of sight, disappearing into the horizon, mesmerizing in its seemingly magical disappearance.

Alone.

She thumbed her wedding ring in absentminded play, the sweat beginning to seep out of her skin, causing the band to roll freely around her finger. She looked at it, its jewel sparkling, shining in the rays streaming through the glass.

At different times through the years she thought of it as her dis-engagement ring. A symbol that marked the last day Jack pursued her. Focused his attention on her. Prioritized her.

This trip was another vain attempt to rekindle something, anything.

Her eyes scanned the vast expanse of sky surrounding her. There it was: her loneliness personified in earthly form.

Inside she found a little happiness in seeing Jack squirm about the car breaking down. He always portrayed confidence, maybe a little arrogance. He seemed to act like he always had the answers for everything, even when she knew he had no clue what he was talking about. Seeing him in situations that ruffled his feathers brought her a little joy. Sick joy, but joy nonetheless.

Laura picked up her cell phone again and tapped some buttons. Nothing.

She threw it back in her purse on the floor. She took some Chap-Stick from one of the pockets and casually put some on, the wax soothing her drying lips. She dug through the bottom of her bag for anything—a stick of gum, a mint, something to soothe her restlessness. But for all the collection of knickknacks it contained, she couldn't find anything.

It was getting hotter in the car, even with the door open.

Her legs, above the knee and below her shorts, were getting hot, exposed to the sun coming through the windshield. She turned sideways in the seat, gazing back down the highway, the way Jack had wandered off. She could see a faint silhouette in the distance, distorted by the heat waves coming off the asphalt. Jack. His shape appearing as a small speck in a funhouse mirror.

Life had been in a perpetual holding pattern for her for years now, so she accepted this current state of boredom with veteran experience. They had been married for five long, slow years. Laura thought that she would have a child or two by now, living the suburban dream of playdates and minivans. But as with all things involving her life with Jack, the family timeline fell on his schedule. He had pushed off having kids until he was more established in his career. She had consented. But then that establishment was always moved further down the line. One more raise, one more promotion . . . yes, someday everything would be fine. And so she waited.

But why? When had she become the clichéd silent wife, the person whom she and her girlfriends raged against in their youth? Had she been born submissive, or just deteriorated into the role, finding the spot of least resistance more comfortable, easy?

Laura felt the dreams of her life slowly decay as time went on, apathy growing as the rust set in. Numbness. The inability to be sparked to action by desires. The loneliness.

Suddenly she wanted him back, back in the car with her, as if she became acutely aware of the magnitude of the situation. Seeing him down the road, a tiny shade in an infinite space of rock and shrub, made her feel exposed. Unsettled. Made her realize her own sense of frailty.

The shadow increased in size, and she could tell he was walking back to the car. As he got closer she could see his shoulders hanging low. Dejected. Worried. A countenance she had not seen very much, and which fit him like an oversized suit. Laura wasn't sure what to make of it; she was just glad he was coming back.

"Why do you have to do these things?" Laura asked as he got back into the car.

"What things?"

"Always having to push it?"

"I don't know."

"We could've just gone to Red Rock Canyon."

"I know."

"Or the dam, we could have done that."

"Yes, we could have."

"What's to see out here?"

"Looks like nothing."

"What are we going to do?"

"I don't know," he said.

"You better think of something."

Jack melted back into the seat. "I know."

7

Molly sat in the cave.

The cave.

How did she ever come to this?

With her cracked knuckles, she massaged her torn ankle that chaffed under the metal restraint. The cuff was attached to a chain that ran across the floor and was anchored to the stone wall. Her shoulders were sore from pulling against it. Pulling, pulling, until exhaustion fell upon her. Her spirits dashed, then revived, and she would pull again. The chain held fast. She pulled some more.

She rubbed her hands together, doing her best to exorcise the stiffness in her fingers. Focusing her mind on the slender digits. Forgetting her surroundings by the momentary sensation of kneading muscle.

Molly looked at her hand, her right one, the hand that she had dug into the side of her kidnapper's neck and clawed for vengeance. The nails were broken and the cuticles were stained with remnants of her own blood. Underneath, the raw abrasions glowed pink, bare tissue left on the links of the chain.

She thought she was tougher, smarter. She thought she was invincible when she set off from home, leaving behind her the dull surroundings and princess bed, the boring life of suburbia. She thought she knew the world. She thought she owned it.

But now she sat in darkness, staring at her flaking flesh as it slowly fell from her hands. Hands that were softer than she ever admitted they were. Molly brought them to her face and cried. She cried not so much in fear of her situation, of the unknown future dreamt in the mind of her captor. She cried as she mourned the death of who she thought she was. The street-smart, thick-skinned renegade.

She had fought in the truck, she told herself. Fought hard. The man seemed generally surprised when she drove her fingers at his throat. He had nearly lost control of the truck, swaying between lanes into oncoming traffic. Sending exhaust into a sea of gawkers on the strip. But he had recovered quickly and punched her across the head. She had never been hit before, and the shock of the pain made her lose her grip. He then grabbed her by the back of the neck and shoved her face into the dashboard. That was all she remembered, waking up alone in the cave chained to the wall.

Molly thought about that moment. She isolated it in her mind. The moment her fingers grabbed on to his neck and clenched. His look of shock. The feeling of control over an uncontrollable situation. It had been brief, a split second, but it gave her strength.

She came out of her recollection and centered herself.

Wincing as her tender hands gripped the chain again . . . she began to pull.

Forty-two. That was the number of striped lines Jack counted down the center of the road before they blurred in the distance. Forty-two. Was there some secret code to be deciphered from that number? Seven squared? No, that was forty-nine. Forty-two. Perfect number times imperfect number. Forty-two, the ultimate answer to everything.

He stared at the charging horse on the steering wheel. Mane and tail blown back, racing west with reckless abandon. Now, all the horses were silent. The Mustang sat grazing on gravel and asphalt.

Jack checked his watch. 3:13 p.m. Another number. Probably some Scripture verse talking about the end of the world, telling him how he was in this mess by his own hand. No matter how many times he checked his iPhone, it remained dead.

He would give his left arm for a "get out of the desert" app right now.

Laura sat in the passenger seat quietly. She was lost in a day-dream, staring at the mountains. Her skin glistened in the sun. She hadn't spoken for a while, and Jack was fine with this. She was upset when he had returned to the car, but now her mood had shifted down several degrees.

They waited.

Jack remembered seeing a movie a couple years back where a

couple went scuba diving off the coast of Florida. They reemerged to find their boat gone, and they were left to drift in the open ocean, waiting for help to come. It never did. He remembered sitting in the theater, chomping on his popcorn, enjoying the spectacle of other people's misery from the comfort of his seat. Now he knew what that couple had felt. He wondered if people would watch his story with the same enthused detachment.

Periodically they would take turns getting out of the car to walk up and down the road, as if by some physical effort they could will a traveler into existence. Their eyes scanned the horizon repeatedly for any sign of life but always came up with the same outcome.

They were completely alone.

Laura watched as Jack walked away from the car down the shoulder. He walked deflated. She had not seen this gait in a long time.

At times during their marriage, she would struggle to remember who he was. He had changed so much in the time they were together. But that is how life rolls itself out. Yes, he had changed, but perhaps the grief arose out of the fact that she had too.

In her mind she would remember what seemed like simpler days, days when they felt connected. Her mind would do her the service of forgetting the destitution they went through and painted the memory in watercolor, fooling herself into believing that the past was without hardship. But things did used to be different. The man walking down the road was still redeemable, she thought. She hoped. And so she quietly supported him with the belief that he would return when the stresses of modern life unburdened themselves from his shoulders. He would return someday and take her dreams into consideration.

And besides, the bitterness left her cold, isolated.

Laura would think of her mother and how she would sit at the table waiting for her father to come home, sometimes with the slight scent of bourbon on his breath, and set his plate down before him as if she had just cooked it. She would sit there waiting for him to talk to her, but he rarely did. Her father's voice in her childhood home had been as rare as his presence. About ten years ago he had got the cancer and told her mother that he loved her dearly. Her mother wept and held his hand in the hospital as he died. After a lifetime of loneliness, that was all she needed.

In her youth she had secretly resented her mother for passively supporting her father. Resented her for being the Xeroxed copy of June Cleaver. A woman without her own dreams.

A woman that she herself had now slowly evolved into.

The duty that her mother had performed all those quiet years now fell on her. Jack provided the means of living but had become detached from enjoying it. Had pushed her to the edges of his attention. She lived her life like she now sat in the car, watching him drift off, hoping on his return that something would spark his soul into seeing her there and smile. Her heart would rise as he would get back into the car, and then slowly rappel down again when his silence filled the empty spaces.

10

Jack would watch Laura walk down the shoulder and back to the car. She would always stop at the same spot. Line twenty-three. Michael Jordan's number. Why twenty-three? After a while he wanted to scream from his seat in the car for her to go farther just for the sake of doing something different, but he held his tongue. She was habitual that way. Her gait shortened with each passing turn and he could see the exhaustion setting in on her. This silent sufferer.

After the initial tongue lashing when Jack got back to the car from his first exploration, the couple passed a few hours talking lightly. Conversations flow that way in times of distress. Lightheartedness is the way of the mind to buffer the soul from impending doom, until it can no longer hold back the dam. Then the darkest thoughts flow in, wiping away all hope and courage. Jack held out longer than Laura, but he eventually succumbed to reality.

At different times he would look over at Laura and see her quietly crying.

11

5:27. This time he walked completely out of sight of the car. Past stripe forty-two. They continued on unceasing. From his perch in the car, he had thought the world ended on stripe forty-two, so thoroughly had his mind convinced him of this, but no. The road just continually drifted on. Its termination point now beyond his imagination. He ventured on to eighty-four and stopped. No use going any farther. No significance in counting.

He turned back to the car and suddenly felt exposed, as if he was being watched. He looked around, but could see nothing. It was the feeling of turning off the basement light and becoming acutely aware of the blackness as a person walks up the stairs. Suddenly he wanted to get back to the safety of the Mustang oven. He walked briskly, almost at a trot, until his heat-wasted muscles halted him.

What was he doing? Imagining things? There was nothing out here. Complete and absolute nothingness. He felt comforted and courageous when he hit line forty-two.

Jack walked back toward the car and for a moment thought that Laura wasn't there, but soon he could make out her face through the windshield. His source of guilt. The gaunt face staring back at him. He got back in the driver's seat and rested his legs.

The water was running low and they had finished the bag of stale chips hours ago. His stomach started cramping, and he could not tell if it was hunger pangs or his intestines slowly constricting in knots of dehydration.

"Jack, how much water do we have left?"

"One bottle."

"That's not that much."

"I know."

"I'm thirsty."

"Here, have a little bit."

"Okay."

He watched her as she took a short drink. He wanted to rip the bottle from her hands and chug every last drop. She handed it to him for his turn, but he put the cap back on. He was keeping score in his mind. Preserving his share of the twenty ounces until the end. Hoarding.

"I'm so hot."

"I know."

Silence filled the vacuum between them.

"I'm scared, Jack," she whispered.

"I know."

The police station outside of Goodwell was of modest construction, built on the cheap. Two desks filled the open interior, a small two-drawer by the front door and a larger metal one in the back next to the sole window. Two fans helped circulate the air that struggled through the vents, pushed along by a decrepit air-conditioning unit.

A vintage cell sat to one side, its swinging door left open. There was hardly ever a reason to close it, even when it was occupied with the occasional drunk. "Best to leave it open and let 'em get to the bathroom" were the words of the police chief who had taken up residence at the big desk several decades ago.

He went by the name Red, even though he didn't have red hair, and his skin was a dark, leathery tan rather than of Indian descent. No one really knows why that name stuck to him, it just did.

He had passed the sixty-year mark awhile back—how long ago was anybody's guess—but he still had the strength of his youth in his body, which was not fit, yet not all soft.

The desk where he sat was light of paperwork, as nothing really happened out this way. And that was the way Red liked it best. There were two framed photographs sitting next to the phone: his wife, who had died ten years earlier, and an old black-and-white picture of Red and two of his buddies from the war. Red stood between the two shirtless Marines, wearing a dirty white T-shirt, the modesty his mother taught him following him all the way to Khe Sanh. The pictures were all he had left of the three people in them.

Across the room sat James, a local kid turned cop, who was decades past a kid. Tall and wiry, James had never fully grown into his body. A bit on the timid side for Red at times, but he was simple and honest, did what he was told, and could be trusted for even the most mundane task.

Two old farts growing old together in misery's outpost.

James looked back at Red. "Sure is hot today, eh, Red?"

"Just like every day I suppose."

"Said it's supposed to be up past 115 today."

"Yup."

James stood up and looked out the front door. Same barrenness, same view. "Well, I guess I might as well go make a round. Not much here to do."

Red glanced up from the papers he was reading. "Take it easy, James."

"I will. Probably swing in and see Gladys, see what she has on tap for today."

Gladys ran the local greasy spoon, the only restaurant in Goodwell.

"Tell her I said hi."

"Will do, Red." James grabbed his hat and opened the front door. The heat from outside slapped his face and took his breath away.

"Man, that's hot," he mumbled as he stepped into the furnace, causing Red to chuckle at his deputy.

Red had another deputy out on the road, Officer PJ Morey. She was young and pretty and did not fit in with James and him. Sugar to his overcooked jerky. He didn't really need another cop out here, but as a favor to PJ's old man, he took her in so she wouldn't go looking for a job in Vegas. Officer Morey was the bright spot in Red and James's day, even though they would never admit it to anyone. She brought a sliver of happiness to the dry desert boredom.

The radio on James's desk came to life, and Red got up to answer it.

"Red, you there?" said a feminine voice, trying to sound harder than was possible.

"Here, PJ. What you got going on?"

"Not much. Nobody's out today. Too hot, I guess."

"You're not going to make your quota then?" Red joked.

"I guess not. James out?"

"Yeah, he's heading over to get some free food. You should join him."

"Gladys's air-conditioning working today?"

"Yup."

"Sounds good. You should join us, Red."

Red smiled at himself at the foolish notion that he was getting asked out. "Naw, you two relax over there. I'll see you both tomorrow."

"All right."

He strolled back over to his desk and sat back down, staring blankly out the window at the western desert and mountain range.

Yup, it sure was a hot one today.

Just like any other day.

8:31. The heat beat down on the rental car with the rage of the devil himself. The doors were open, the power windows worthless shields against the occasional sand devil. The hot desert air blew through the car, giving no comfort. The only respite was the black ragtop, which at least kept the direct rays from burning the couple's skin, but it also baked them at a slow roast.

The setting sun over the western mountains brought both a feeling of gladness that the sauna would ease, and fear that, despite stewing for almost a full day, not a single car had passed by. Jack and Laura were now stripped down to their underwear, sweat rolling off their bodies in slow streams; their life seeping from them with the steady cadence of a dripping faucet.

"I'm sure someone will come by, I'm sure of it," Jack whispered, trying his best to believe his own words.

"You said that hours ago," Laura replied, not opening her eyes. She kept them shut all the time now.

"Yeah, I did."

Jack had no energy to encourage her to keep up hope. He had none for himself. Hope is not boundless. What is given to others depletes one's own stock, as if in the giving, the other's despair is exchanged in return. Strength must be given. It is not self-manufactured. It is a gift. Jack's supply was almost gone. Laura's had vanished hours earlier.

He sat there and thought about a time when he was in grad school. Jack had an instructor who rode his butt harder than any person he'd ever met. Nothing he did and no amount of preparation could quell the fire of the professor's condescension. Jack had wanted to quit.

Laura was the rock then. She encouraged him to keep pushing, and with her strength he had succeeded. Very rarely had he viewed her as the strong one. He had forgotten that time until now, all these years later. He wore his degrees like badges of honor, thinking himself a self-made man. Was he?

He glanced over at her and noticed that she appeared to be sleeping. He didn't know why, but he was struck by an acute sense of loneliness. He reached over and nudged her arm. She stirred but did not wake up.

"Hon?"

"Hmm," she groaned.

"I love you."

"I know."

The sun dipped below the western mountain, and shadows stretched their fingers eastward across the valley. The shade bathed the car and Jack felt the relief on his skin. Night was coming and still no sign of life. He looked at Laura, sitting right next to him. He felt scared. Alone. Weak. He feared for himself like the coward the school yard bully always thought he was.

He looked down at his watch. It too had stopped. 9:15. Some meaning in this? Perhaps the time the coroner would presume that they both ceased to be.

14

Punching through the desert night, the black pickup truck drove with abandon through the badlands' dust, kicking up a jet of sand and rock. The dim headlights fought to illuminate the path ahead, but Colten was driving on instinct. He knew this trail. He had been out here a long time. Waiting like a prisoner before the parole board who knew that no reprieve was ever in the cards, savoring the denials like a fine wine. Relishing in absolute abjection.

He drove on toward the western hills. It was a hike from the gas station in Goodwell, and he fought with himself constantly about the need to keep up the charade. It was as good an outpost as any. He felt exposed in the bigger cities. It was always a risk to go fishing there.

No, Goodwell was the right choice. His hick exterior blended in well, and his choices were limited.

He passed the trail's termination point and proceeded on the ruts grooved by many passes of the truck. No one ever came out here. It was off the map, right in the crease of the fold that a traveler couldn't adjust their eyes to. Objection left his mind. This was right where he was supposed to be. For now.

The two-track up the mountain was cut from the rock. A slithering gouge, wide enough for his truck, that snaked up the mountain from the desert floor. The road ended in a clearing encircled by sheer walls of gray limestone, streaked sporadically with layers of blood-red sandstone. The folding veins of the earth.

He stopped the truck and killed the engine. Walking toward the rock, he went into a small cave above the valley. The air parted in front of him like a bowing servant as he made his way to the back . . . where she was.

Molly huddled in the back, silent, her legs pulled up against her chest. Her hair hung about her like the burnt wings of an angel as she watched him enter the hollow. He dropped a bottle of water and a packaged pastry by her feet and walked to the other side of the cave, where he stood looking at her. She grabbed the water and downed it quickly, only realizing when it was gone that she should have rationed it.

"I want to go home," she whispered.

"Naw, you don't want that."

She ran the pastry through her bleeding fingers, wondering if by eating it she would in a sense become obligated for the food. She was thankful that she had not been violated as of yet, but the future kept fear in her chest.

"Why are you doing this?" she asked, not really wanting to know the answer.

He lit a cigarette, and the smoke made the unbreathable catacomb toxic.

"Why? Ain't no sense asking why. Why'd you run out here? Don't matter, does it. Point is, you're here. Right now."

"I want to go home," she repeated, a bit more assertive than the first time.

"You sure they want you back? You ran off. Cut that thread good and clean. Huh, they probably don't want you back. Probably sitting together right now thinking, 'Glad she's gone.'"

She thought of them. Her mom, the classic suburbanite profile. Her father, successful and boring. Why had she felt so smothered by them? What fake disdain had she groomed in her heart to the point of becoming real? Their love was overbearing. Smothering goodness that she ran from. For freedom. For this. Perhaps Colten was right. Perhaps she could not go home again. Too much time had passed, she had come too far to ever go back, she thought. Too far to walk back into the house and expect them to hold her again, to accept her back into the fold.

Colten suspected he knew her thoughts. Walking over to the girl, he crouched down to stare at her, basking in the hopelessness that came pulsating through her pores. He puffed in a toke and held it until his lungs ached for release. He cocked his head to the side and blew out the smoke.

The girl stared back at him, pursed her lips, and spit in his face.

Cole's reaction was pure reflex. He backhanded her across her face, sending her reeling against the rock. The girl whimpered slightly and then composed herself again. She did not want to give Cole the satisfaction of making her cry, though her cheek stung something fierce. She brought her eyes back to bear on his face.

"What are you going to do to me?"

"Nothing you don't want."

"I don't want this."

"What do you want then?"

"I want to go home," she whispered, her voice cracking.

"Naw, we both know you don't want that."

15

Jack awoke to a dark night where the stars burned like orphans in a field of black. He did not remember falling asleep. He looked over at Laura, who was in the reclined seat next to him. He touched her arm, but she didn't move. The skin was warm but lifeless. He sat up more with a quick start and said her name. She groaned a bit and then fell back into sleep. Jack grabbed the last water bottle, which held a thimbleful of moisture in its base, unscrewed the cap, and poured a small amount into his wife's mouth. It sat there between her parched lips, but she did not drink.

Jack looked at her, but his mind was too fatigued to process any solution. They were dying, and he knew it. He accepted it now. His only wish was that Laura would sleep through it. Why awake to this horror again? He envied her in dreamland. He did not remember the last time he envied her.

The car door opened with a squeak and Jack stepped out onto the blacktop. The heat still nipped at his ankles, but the air was cooler. He had no idea what time it was.

Jack thought himself an interesting sight for any animal that might be lurking off the highway. He staggered half dazed in his sandals and his boxers toward the center line, then turned around, hoping, praying for a sign of life. There was none. No haze of city light, no moving headlights in the distance. Just moonlight, stars, and heat. If he could have spared the water, he would have cried.

Here he was, reduced to a loincloth in the middle of nowhere, forced to watch his wife die a slow death by heat exhaustion, only to follow close behind. Yet his mind could not accept his fate. He still hoped for rescue. He still hoped that he was watching a movie, and all he had to do was wait for the credits to roll and the lights to click on and be ushered out.

His legs collapsed and he slumped to the road. The tar singed the back of his legs, but he didn't struggle. What was the use? By daybreak he wouldn't have the strength to beat back the sun. The heat would slowly cook him and he would die. He prayed that they would go quickly. Before the tearing and the ripping of the coyotes and birds.

How quickly they had come to this. Just this morning, they were happy to leave the strip, content that they would be back by midafternoon and play in the pool, have a nice dinner, enjoy the city. The idea that they would die on a highway seemed ludicrous. But here they were.

"I don't deserve this," Jack repeated to himself.

He reached down and felt the dimpled surface of the road. Why build such a thing? Jack thought about the day laborers who must have poured their sweat into laying the road. So much work for a road going nowhere. Why bother? Who traveled this narrow, deathly stretch of earth that they would require pavement?

Why does a dark road grip the heart in fear? When on foot, a person quickens their pace at night as fears of stalking boogeymen come haunting up behind them. A flash of headlights causes the muscles to tense in anticipation of complete terror. What is coming? Jack stared off into the night, looking at the faded yellow lines vanish in the darkness. Forty-two was buried in blackness.

He would have killed for that sensation of anticipating the approach of a stranger. At least that would have meant discovery. But there were no boogeymen out tonight.

"Jack? Jack?" Laura groaned from the car, sounding scared and exhausted. "Jack!"

He crawled over to the door and climbed into the driver's seat. "I'm here . . . I'm here."

She still had not opened her eyes. "I thought you left me, I thought . . ."

"I'm here. Go back to sleep, hon."

She drifted off into space as he sat there looking at her. The pain gripped his heart and tore his soul.

"I don't deserve this," he whispered, "I don't deserve this."

Soon, darkness took him too.

It may have been the slow tapping on the windshield that woke him, or it may have been the sudden feeling of his soul's first attempt to leave his body. It took a moment for his eyes to focus, the moonlight shading the inside of the car a subtle hue of crypt-like eeriness. It was still night and his head hurt. What time was it? Jack tried to rub the sleep from his eyes but could barely lift his hands and succeeded more in slapping his face. Once conscious, he looked out the front of the car.

On the windshield a spider the size of Jack's fist sat staring back at him. Its hairy legs tapping on the glass in slow, rhythmic staccato. They stared at each other. The only two beings on earth locked in a silent gaze, Jack now fully awake. The tapping stopped. The beast content in its work.

Jack glanced over to his left. The door was still open from when he had crawled in after his journey to the center line. The spider seemed to follow Jack's eyes, realizing the car was open for inspection. It looked at the open door and stretched its legs. It slowly stalked across the glass with silent footfalls to the doorjamb, its front legs feeling its way.

Jack lost sight of the creature in the jamb. But he knew it was coming. Soon, two legs moved through the air like antennae listening for sound. Slowly, the spider reached into the car and pulled itself inside. Its thick black body pulled along by its hairy legs.

Jack's heart stopped as he watched it inch its way onto the dash, resting in between the steering wheel and the windshield.

It resumed its staredown of Jack now from the vinyl shelf inside the car, studying him with what seemed to be a hundred eyes. Jack sat paralyzed. Fear gripped him as hard as he gripped the seat he was sitting on.

His breath was now labored. He tried to remember every Discovery Channel show he ever watched. He was sure this thing had come to devour them whole. To wrap them up Frodo Baggins–style and pull them back to its lair.

The spider turned and scurried over to the passenger side, onto the door, and slipped down onto Laura's leg. It sat there looking back at Jack, rubbing its forelegs together, preparing to dig in.

He was powerless. Does he scream her name? Wake her up? Sit there and watch this thing bite into her leg? It sat there for an eternity, and then it moved slowly toward Jack.

Creeping ever so stealthily, it moved across Laura's bare legs and reached for the center console. Its eight legs stretched across the cup holder as its body sank into it.

He could jump out of the car back onto the road. But could this thing jump too? Would it leap after him? What if Laura woke up and saw that he had left her there with that thing squatting next to her? He was in full-blown panic mode, indecisive, as his heart did its best to force itself out of his rib cage.

The spider moved across the center console and onto Jack's thigh. He shut his eyes and waited for the thing to strike. The anticipation was killing him.

Just do it! he thought, but the spider just sat there. *Do it!*

The bug moved again, across Jack's other leg, and headed out the door. Jack watched as it hit the pavement and scurried off across the road. He shut the door with all the strength he could muster. The sweat poured off his face, the last of what fluid remained in his body. He looked over at Laura, who slept, oblivious to the events that had just slithered across her body. His body loosened and he passed out.

17

Morning light skirted the eastern ring of the valley as gently as an Easter sunrise.

"Jack," she whispered.

"Yeah?"

"Jack . . . water?"

"No."

"It's all gone?"

"Yeah," he said.

"Oh."

"Sorry."

"Okay."

They drifted in a daze between waking and oblivion.

"Jack?"

"Yeah?"

"I thought you left."

"Nope."

"Okay."

It must have been early afternoon when Jack heard sounds outside the car. His strength was gone and he could not open his eyes. He was completely wasted. It sounded like a clomping on concrete, and then a slow huff of air forced out of huge nostrils. He cracked his eyelid and was blinded by sunlight. He had no strength to move his head, was barely able to comprehend the images in his peripheral vision. He thought he could see a horse in the passenger side mirror, but then the door swung open.

Jack could hear rustling in the passenger seat as someone reached in, grabbed Laura, and lifted her out of the car. The door was kicked shut and he could see again in the mirror. A man lifted Laura and draped her across the back of the horse. Then he was gone from view and Jack was left looking at his wife slung like a bag of mail across the animal's back.

The driver's side door swung open and a shadow fell across Jack's face. A hand grabbed his chin and turned it toward the door. Water poured into his mouth.

"You awake?" a voice boomed.

Jack could only muster a grunt.

"Drink some more. I'm leaving you a bottle. My horse can't carry you both. I'll be back. You awake?"

Jack could feel himself being shaken. "Y . . . yes."

"Good . . . I'll be back. Don't go dying on me."

And with that, the car door slammed shut. Staring at the passenger side mirror, Jack watched the man, horse, and Laura disappear. He had no idea what had just happened. No strength to get up and follow, no strength to care if a mountain man had just come down and stolen his wife. No strength to care about anything. With his eyes now open, he looked down at the water bottle placed between his legs. He struggled to lift it, but it seemed to weigh a thousand pounds. With all his strength, he lifted it to his mouth. Water spilled down his lips onto his chest. The coolness startled his senses and he dropped the bottle, its contents pouring out onto the floorboard. He had not the strength to pick it up. He did not care anymore.

Staring out the windshield, Jack looked down the two-lane blacktop. The heat rose off the pavement like waves of water drifting in limbo, obscuring the base of the mountains an unknown number of miles away. He watched as it moved, hypnotized by the cadence of the desert ocean. The convection slowly reached out to him, lapping at the ground, moving closer and closer. He stared.

Then they slowly appeared. First, one dancing shadow moved its way into reality, followed by others. They sat there at the bend of the road blinking at the car. Could they see him? Were they really there? They moved with the waves, performing a slow dance of twisted matter. The leader was larger than the rest. His form was liquid, shape shifting with the air and the other shadows around him.

The silence intensified inside the car. Jack could hear his breath, his heartbeat inside his ears. The wind gently blowing across the road. They looked at him. From miles down the road, he could tell they were sizing him up. The breeze intensified and the shadows danced. They began to whip themselves up into a slow fury, like teenagers in a mosh pit. Battering each other, the shadows moved; some baring enigmatic teeth and devouring the shape next to them, only to have the victim materialize again. But the one kept staring, refusing to be jostled from its position.

His heart beat a steady cadence and the shadows moved with it. The cloud drifted slowly toward the car, churning like a thunderhead. It crept closer and closer in a macabre cabaret. The breeze shifted and intensified, blowing the shadows closer with each passing second. The one leading, with the others wrestling in its wake. Jack counted off their approach with each disappearing center stripe of the road. The mountains in the distance became obscured as they now took on a more solid composure. Faster, faster, his heart raced as their pace quickened.

Lions zeroing in on the kill, running.

Faster and faster, their frenzy growing more rapid with each step.

They hit the car with the force of an earthquake and the sound of a whisper. The sun was eclipsed, and the only thing Jack could hear as he blacked out was the sound of his own muffled scream.

19

Her knees were tucked up under her chin, her arms wrapped around her legs, slowly rocking.

Her eyes searched for bearing but she was blind. Too long in the dark now. How many days? She didn't know.

Molly could feel the rock wall to her back, the warm stone underneath her.

Silent movements stirred the air around her, and occasionally she could feel a presence grace the hair on her bare arms. A haunted breeze, a slow exhaling of foul wind.

The cell, for that is how she thought of it, was silent to everything but her heartbeat. She could hear the blood flow through the veins in her neck up into her head. The slow, rhythmic beat of life. The air stirred with the beat, jumping pace when she was startled by the graze of the unseen shadows.

She thought about how she had come here. Not the mechanics of the fact; she recalled that all too well. But rather all the nuanced steps that she had taken, all the seemingly small choices that spiraled out of control and landed her in oblivion. She thought of her mom with her heavy hand of practical suburban life. She had yearned to live freer, to do what she wanted, to make decisions for herself. That is where the dream had started. She had longed to live without restraint, not realizing she was incapable of living without support.

In the dark she could feel her tears moisten the skin on her forearms and run to the crease in her elbow where they pooled and evaporated. Vapor gone before their existence could be noticed by the ones that came after them. Much like herself, she thought. Gone before actually living.

The shadow breaths moved with her despairing thoughts. Suicide had never been in her vocabulary, but with each drip of a tear, with each whiff of silent shade, the dark thoughts would pop into her mind like a twisted whack-a-mole game. She worked to beat one down, to have another thought take its place, taunting her with sarcastic laughing.

She grieved for her shattered image.

Why did she do this? She could see the vision of home in her mind. The day she packed her backpack and headed out the front door. She could feel the coolness of the brass handle in her palm. *Stop, turn around!* she thought as she watched the scene in her memory, but her doppelganger simply closed the door and walked down the driveway, an impish grin on her face and invincibility nestled in her back pocket. She watched herself disappear down the street and mourned. Despair, regret, and shame swam in the deep pools of her memories.

The shadows were her only companions.

PART TWO

THE CABIN

If a soul walked west into the wasteland of the Mojave, and kept walking until all hope of finding civilization had been lost, dehydration had turned the brain to a mushy paste, and fear had given way to slow acceptance and welcoming of death, ten steps past this point of utter despair they would find the cabin of Boots.

It was not so much a cabin as it was a trailer with an add-on not designed by any skilled architect. A porch graced the front of the shack, and its exterior was patched together with an odd assortment of material. The tin roof was beaten with age and shimmered in the desert sun.

The yard, if rocks and sand could be called such, sprouted a few resilient weeds that clawed for life between the stone and eked out a meager existence. The property line was undefined and could have stretched for miles toward the western mountains, which offered a spectacular view.

Around back, there was a small pen and horse stable suitable for its lone inhabitant, a brown-and-white pinto of questionable disposition. Clouds of dust fell after each footfall as the mare sauntered back and forth between its water trough and the pen rail.

South of the pen and pushed a little farther out was a small cemetery plot with washed-out stones of memorial. A family plot it seemed, the names of which were now lost to time. Broken souls who may have given up hope of ever finding paradise now resting their bones among the sun-soaked stones.

The cabin itself offered little comfort of modern life. It contained a single bedroom with a small nightstand. There was no plumbing out here in the wasteland, so the decrepit bathroom off the hallway only served to mock an anxious bladder. A homemade lean-to outside provided a primitive solution.

Through the front door was the open living space that served as a kitchen, dining area, and living room, all in Spartan fashion. The owner of the place never bothered to clean, as the desert winds just blew more dust in through the open windows before a broom could make a dent. The only decoration apart from the candle sconces was a framed picture next to the door. The sketch inside was similar to what a young Ansel Adams would have hung on his mother's refrigerator.

There was no power out here, no television, no reception on any radio if Boots had bothered owning one. The kitchen had a hand pump that brought cool water up from a deep well and made the residency of the cabin even possible. Though the sun beat down with a vengeance, the air in the hut was cool, as if the sun dared not cross the threshold. This was the place that Boots brought the couple he had saved from death on the deserted road.

He was a small man, old and weathered by the sun. His beard was long and hung to the middle of his chest, and though not white, the gray mixed with the black of its natural color to form a mop that hung from his chin. His teeth were not holding well against the years of neglect but still supported him fully in chewing whatever he may need to chew, especially when it came to his pouch of tobacco.

His western shirt sported the timeless fashion of the discount thrift store, and the only point of pride in his dress were his ranch hand Nocona boots. A philosopher once said that "a man's feet must be planted in his country, but his eyes should survey the world," and Boots was sure that his shoes planted him firmly on his piece of earth, and his view of the Mojave was splendid.

He looked at the two people who now occupied his cabin. The woman was resting on the couch. The man was back on the bed. Boots began spreading his backwater healing on them with patience and purpose. The woman had seemed in dire straits when she first arrived, but she was recovering quickly. The man, however, continued to thrash in a fevered state. Cold compresses from the water pump were refreshed every half hour or so, and the only break Boots took was to enjoy a dip on the front porch. He refused to chew in his house. "Man's gotta have standards," he always said.

The woman began to stir out of delirium and opened her eyes. She was startled by the desert nomad staring back at her.

"What . . . who are you?" the woman whispered.

"I'm Boots, and you're going to be all right. Just rest there. Ain't no use trying to get up."

She nestled down and drifted between waking and sleep, unsettled as if haunted by a dream.

Boots walked to the back room and tried to pour some water into the man's stomach, but he would have none of it. Again, with the same elderly patience, Boots worked to break the man's fever, to cool his raging body temperature and bring him back to the land of the living.

Man is not made for the desert. The sun slowly begins to cook the organs inside the body. Cramps and exhaustion rack the muscles. Insanity creeps in as the body temperature rises. Corpses have been found along the border where illegal immigrants have tried to claw the skin off their bodies in a vain attempt at cooling their internal thermostats. It is not pleasant when the baked man gives up the ghost. Boots worked to make sure that Jack would not join their number.

Laura woke the next morning, and though she still felt nauseated and wiped out, she sat up and placed her feet on the floor. The rug below them spun and then settled down. She looked over to see an old man sitting at a small table just a few feet from her. She jumped back into the couch, clutching the blanket that had slipped down around her waist.

"Wh . . . where am I?"

"This is my place."

"Where's Jack?"

"Jack? That his name? He's in the back bed. Don't worry about him. He's coming along. Not as quickly but just as surely."

"Good." Laura felt her muscles relax. Something in the old man's voice soothed her anxiety, and though she didn't think of herself as naïve, she felt as if she had little to fear from the stranger sitting across from her. "You're . . . Boots, right?"

He nodded. "You've been through a lot, it looks like."

The man got up and retrieved a fresh glass of water for her. She looked at the cool liquid floating in the aged Mason jar and sipped it slowly.

"You drink that slow now, no need throwing up on my rug."

"All right."

The old man sat back in his chair and eyed her, looking her over as if she was born from a different species than himself. Laura stared down into her glass, sensed his eyes probing. Her mind checked the myriad of feelings in her body, but she felt assured that she was unharmed. Waking up in a strange man's trailer got her thoughts to racing, but she quickly reassured herself that she had not been messed with.

She looked over at Boots sitting in his chair and saw a sense of contentment in his eyes, empty of malice, but not entirely sure if madness didn't creep in around the pupils.

Boots broke the silence. "So, what you two doing way out here?"

"Just driving. The car broke down. We didn't see anyone."

"Don't see much out here"—he smiled—"that's why it's called *out here.*"

Boots chuckled at his own joke and Laura smiled with him, despite her pounding head. "Well, thank you. I thought we were goners."

"Don't mention it. You two were in a bad spot. Least I could do."

Laura forced another mouthful of water down her throat. The coolness soothed the soreness for a moment. "So where's here?"

"Here's kinda between the cracks, about as far away as you can get from crazy folk. Don't worry, I'll get you where you need to be in a short while."

"Do you have a phone?" she asked, looking around the room for any sign of technology.

"Ain't got no phone out here. Naw, I don't need all that stuff. Out here you gotta rely on yourself. Jack will be all right. Fever looks to be breaking. And you, well, you're coming around just fine."

"Shouldn't we get a doctor?"

"Naw, y'all be fine. Seen it before. Yeah, you'll be just fine."

"My head hurts."

"It will for a bit. Gotta get the water back in you is all."

She set the glass on the table in front of her and her head swam. In the pit of her stomach, she felt the growl of hunger pains and tried to think about the last time she had food. It seemed like a different lifetime.

"Do you have anything to eat?" she asked.

"Sure do," he said.

Boots got up and fixed a small plate of rations on the table for her. It was mystery food to be sure, but the aroma smelled fine and the fact that Laura's taste buds felt burnt out of her mouth made the meal palatable. She was not about to complain.

After eating, she settled back on the couch and napped off and on. Sometimes she would open her eyes and see Boots busying himself about the kitchen, other times she would be alone in the room. She took water off and on and could feel her body begin to normalize. Nightfall came and she slept soundly.

By the next morning, Laura felt like a new woman.

Time passed without observance. Jack woke in a bed covered by an old patchwork quilt. He felt filthy, as if he had broken a fever and had not showered in weeks. On the battered nightstand next to him was some water and towels. He had no idea how long he had been asleep or any clue as to where he was. He tried to recollect what had happened, but it too seemed like a dream in which he could grasp the sentiment but not the action. His head ached and his muscles screamed as he tried to sit up.

Jack tracked his memories. He remembered driving out into the desert, the car dying. He remembered the spider. How could he forget that? He remembered someone carrying Laura to a horse and taking off.

Laura!

He jumped to his feet despite the pain and opened the bedroom door. Laura sat at a small table in a large room that served as a kitchen and living area. She stared back at him from her plate of pancakes with a look of shock.

"Jack! You're awake!" she said as she ran to him. "Here, let's get some clothes on you."

He was still too weak in the head to have noticed his nakedness, but didn't resist her as she pushed him back into the bedroom. She sat him on the bed and grabbed his clothes.

"Where are we?" he struggled.

"A cabin. This man found us and carried us here. We thought you'd never wake up."

"How long?"

"Four days. Your fever was high. It broke last night and you took a little food."

"Who is he?"

"Just some sweet old-timer. He calls himself Boots." She smiled. "He's got these old leather boots that tap the floor like Gregory Hines. I'm not sure what his real name is."

He slumped back on the bed after she pushed his shirt over his head. "I feel like garbage."

"Come on out and eat something. You need to get your strength back."

Sitting at the table, Jack forced down a pancake. His throat was swollen and his cracked lips bled a little when he tried to chew. He glanced at Laura, who looked little worse for wear by the whole ordeal.

"So where is this guy?"

"He stepped outside about half an hour ago. He said he'd be back soon."

Jack glanced around the cabin. It was something out of a photo shoot for *White Trash Living*. There was no power that he could see. Candles sat in the middle of the table and in sconces on the wall. The kitchen had a single iron tub with a hand pump water faucet. No TV. No telephone.

"This guy doesn't believe in modern living?"

"I don't think so. Doesn't even have a car. Just an old horse. But that horse saved our lives."

"I bet," Jack said, still looking around. "Did he go to get help?"

"I don't think so. I think he just went to get some food for today."

"Hmph."

Jack thought back to the highway. To the feeling of being pulled from the car and poured over the back of an animal. Somewhere in his mind he could feel the sensation of a slow trot and the clicking of hooves, the smell of horse hair and dust. He had no idea how long the walk was, just as he had no idea of how long he had slept. He stared back at Laura, who had a look of contentment on her face.

"You having fun yet?" he asked sarcastically.

"Bunches," she said with a slight grin. "We are very lucky, Jack. We could be dead right now . . ."

"Because of me?"

"If it wasn't for Boots. He saved us."

"Yeah."

"Jack," she whispered, "we are lucky."

He dropped his eyes to the plate. He had almost killed them both, driving into solitude just for curiosity's sake. Jack could see Laura listless in the passenger seat, slowly edging toward death, the result of him wanting to be "John Wayne for the day." That phrase was now eternally etched in his mind. How could he ever forgive himself? How could he come to grips with the fact that he wasn't an adventurer, just a desk jockey whose only skill was punching a time card? He felt like a failure before her. Emasculated. Weak.

"It's all right, we're okay now," she whispered as she reached across the table for his hand.

He let her take it. He hated her at that moment. Laura, the benefactress of his ambition, the one who looked up to him, offering comfort to his brokenness. He hated his whole life in one fell swoop. His mind racing, he almost wished he had died in that car. He let the rage pass before he looked up at her, but before he could speak, the front door opened and Boots walked in.

"So, you're awake. Good," said the man walking through the door. He was an odd specimen for the twenty-first century. He was decked out in a worn western shirt with pearl buttons on the pockets, the plaid pattern worn down to more of solid beige. His denim was as dusty as his boots, which indeed did tap across the wooden floor to the water pump where he washed his hands. He placed his cowboy hat on the counter as he ran water over his head and scrubbed some into his mangy beard. Jack recognized him—from every western and gold rush movie he had ever seen. Here was a walking stereotype of the grizzled mountain man. But what stereotype is not rooted in reality, some subtle gene that pops out like pheromones to explain an object in its essence. This was Boots. Rasputin of no-man's-land.

"What say you, Jack? Getting your strength back?"

"Yes. Thanks, uh, Boots, is it?"

The old man nodded.

"Nice place you have here, Boots," Jack said with a mild tone of condescension.

Laura shot him a look of disapproval that Jack didn't take the time to acknowledge.

"Thanks. It ain't much, but it's mine. Been out here a long time, so it's just broke in to suit. Got anything you would need to scratch a living."

"Got a phone or a car? A way back to town?"

"Don't need that stuff. Ain't ever been in a hurry to get there. I got my horse and she does the trick. You met her already. She can pull her share, but now gets tired right quick. Ain't like she used to be."

The old man sat down at the table, his beard still dripping water onto his shirt. A small bead ran down his forehead. Boots's eyes looked right through Jack as they sat across from each other. The old man's crystal blue irises awash with age. Jack felt uneasy, exposed, like lying on a gurney in a hospital smock as a doctor flipped through charts looking for the diagnosis to an unexplained disease. He didn't like the way this old man made him feel. He could sum that up right away. Something about him just did not seem right.

"How soon till we can leave?"

"Leave? You ready to go already? You just got here," Boots said with a grin.

"Yeah, just ready to get back, you know."

"I'll get you back. Don't worry. Takes some time, I have to make sure you're ready."

Jack was about to lash back when Laura straightened up. "Your call, Boots. We are in your hands." She smiled at Boots and gave a side glance to her husband. He sat there and fumed.

"I guess you are. Naw, desert is a tough spot. Got to plan it right to get y'all home. Besides, can't reckon you can walk more than ten steps before collapsing, Jack. You need to get your gumption up."

"Huh?"

"Horse can't carry us all. Seeing how it's the two of you, you're going to have to walk it out."

Jack looked out the front door that had failed to latch when Boots came in. It slowly swung open, revealing the rolling desert that stretched out before the cabin in unceasing waves. The heat rising from the rock and blurring the horizon. He looked back at his plate but had lost his appetite. He pushed it away as the food he had managed to eat attempted to force its way back up his throat. He had no strength in his body. It had taken all he had to move from the bed to the table. Boots was right. He wouldn't make it ten steps.

"I guess we're your prisoners then," Jack said, masking the truth of his words with a faint laugh.

"If that is how you want it."

The sheriff car pulled up to the gas station in Goodwell. The door opened and Red got out of the car and walked into the store. He took off his hat and wiped his forehead with a handkerchief from his pocket. He walked back to the cooler and grabbed a Coke off the top shelf.

He popped the top as he made his way up to the counter. "How's it going, Cole?"

"Not bad, Red, how about you?"

"Hot. Been a scorcher the past couple a days."

Colten kept flipping through the magazine on hand as the cop took another sip from the can, staring out the window through his Ray-Bans.

A voice through static jumped out of the radio on Red's belt. He responded and listened.

"There ain't nothing out here, boss."

"Where you boys at?"

"Almost up to Sandy Valley. The boys are about ready to call it a day."

"All right."

Colten looked up from his reading. "You looking for something?"

"Looks like bodies now." Red put his radio back and took another swig of Coke.

"How's that?"

"Found a car abandoned out by Shiloh. Nice one. Blue Mustang. Turned out to be a rental from Vegas. Couple from out east rented it a few days ago. James got some of the guys from over at Gladys's to go looking for them."

"Really?"

"Yeah, it seems some fool tried to off-road the sucker. Did a pretty good job of it. Got about fifteen miles off the nearest road."

"Now that don't make much sense, does it, Red?"

"Can't make sense out of these folks, Cole. Probably lost his money in town and wanted to go out in style. Anyways, we're out looking for 'em now. Not sure what we're going to find though."

"Car was empty?"

"Yeah, looks like they got it stuck and then decided to walk it out. Pretty long walk though."

"Well, one thing for sure, you get rid of a fool, three more to take his place." Colten lit up a cigarette with a grin.

"Yup. We'll find 'em sooner or later. Ship 'em back home UPS and all. Anyway, coming from Vegas and ending up past Shiloh, they might have passed through here. You remember seeing folks like that come by?"

"Naw, I don't think so."

"All right," Red said, putting the can down and placing a dollar on the counter. "I better head up there. Make sure them boys haven't turned this into a party. If you think of anything, be sure and let me know."

"You got it, Red."

Colten eyed the police cruiser as it pulled onto the road away from the gas station. It always made him a bit uneasy whenever the cop came into the store, but he was a firm believer in keeping those most threatening close to the vest.

He remembered the incident with Jack a few days before and smiled to himself. *Guy like that, car like that . . . due a beatdown if I ever saw one*. Well, can't get much more beat down than dying of the heat in the Mojave.

Colten took a toke from the cigarette and exhaled with deliberate pleasure.

"I hope you died slow, Jack."

They sat on the bed, Jack rubbing his head with both hands, Laura staring out the small window. He followed her gaze. She was looking at Boots, who was sitting silently on the front porch.

"You could be nicer, Jack."

"Yeah." He started rubbing his head again.

She turned and studied him. "He did save us. At least try to be civil."

"All right."

"It's just sometimes, you can be a little short—"

"Got it!"

Jack stood up. He hated everything in the world at that moment. The air in the bedroom became stifling, and he made for the door. Laura didn't say anything more. He could sense her watching him through the window as he stumbled off the front porch and started walking around the house. He threw a quick glance back at Boots, whose eyes were following him with apathetic detachment.

The cabin was as unremarkable outside as it was in. The yard was nothing as such. Rock and dirt trailed off into the horizon from every side. Out back, there was the pen where the mare loafed, taking turns at the water trough between saunters in the baking sun. Farther back was the post fence with weeds and cacti shooting up sporadically between intentionally placed stones. The cemetery. Jack walked up to the fence and looked out onto the field. A haunting filled his gut.

He thought about the highway.

How close to death had they been? How close had their bones been from being whitewashed in the desert wind's sandblaster? The day out on the blacktop still lingered as a hung-over mystery. He could see it in his mind like snapshots: the road, the water bottle on the floorboard, a horse in a rearview mirror, blackness.

It was the blackness that gnawed at the back of his neck. Hallucination, that's what it must have been. The effects of dehydration. Blindness. But this pit in his stomach suggested that deep down inside, it was something more. He had seen something out there on the highway. Something that flayed him open and exposed all the worst parts of him.

His mind searched like a defragging hard drive, attempting to put the files back together. Just then he heard footsteps approaching behind him and the recall ceased.

"You sure you're fit to be out here? Should be inside resting yourself."

Jack stared off, acknowledging Boots's presence with a slight glance, but not saying a word.

"Not too many folk in there worth the time for talk," Boots said as he stepped beside Jack and nodded toward the grave markers.

Jack looked at him. Was this desert monk a serial killer hoping to add the two of them to his macabre collection of bones? The old man was crazy, Jack was sure of that, but he didn't feel that Boots was *that* crazy.

"Some of them been there a long time. Longer than I've been here. Some I know from way back. No use carrying them way off for the coyotes to get. People knew to keep them close by."

"You kill them yourself?"

"Ha . . . that's a good one, Jack. Naw, ain't no one there by my hand. Different story most of them got. Some caught fever. Others just walked out after eating and gave up the ghost. Only one thing the same in this life. We all end up there."

"How many?"

"Not sure. Some stones ain't got no mark. Some do. Ain't been added to for a long time. People who come out here nowadays die on their own. Sometimes no one finds them. Sometimes they get found. Bones at least. Bones don't tell you much, just that they're alone."

"Sort of insane, isn't it? Having this right next to your house?"

"Naw, ain't insane. Don't get much company out here. And they don't eat much." Boots chuckled. "But like I say, they ain't good at talking."

They stood in silence as the wind picked up and blew heat into their faces.

"What are you two chatting about?" Laura asked as she walked up tentatively to the two men, her hair flowing back behind her, and a subtle bead of sweat sauntered down her temple. Boots's face lit up in the same annoying way that the gas station clerk's had when they stopped in Goodwell.

"Not much, just showing Jack the family album."

"What you got going on here, James?" Red asked as he approached the abandoned car, its blue steel reflecting in the daytime blaze.

James stood stumped. The doors were opened as well as the trunk. Two NHP officers were walking through the brush about a half mile off, searching for any clues about the missing occupants of the vehicle.

"Not much, Red. Car is pretty much empty. A couple empty water bottles is about it. A purse and some cell phones."

"They work?"

"Naw. Dead. Car is dead too. Won't turn over."

Red walked around the vehicle, squatted down, and looked underneath. "Well, it's not hung up. Doesn't look to be stuck on anything. Out of gas?"

"Gauge says three quarters. I opened the tank and could still smell fumes. Just no battery power looks like."

"Strange."

"That it is, Red. The boys over there have been out walking for a while. Ain't found anything. We saw a set of footprints heading back a ways, up that ridge there, but they just double back to the car."

"Any other sign of heading out?"

"Naw," James said as he motioned toward the front of the

Mustang, "wind looks like it swept the valley clean, right up to the car. We didn't find any footprints that way."

"But the ones in back were still there?"

"Yup."

"Huh, convenient place for the wind to stop, don't you think?"

"I guess so . . . didn't really think about it, but yeah, strange."

Red sat down in the driver's seat of the Mustang. The heat from the seat scared his backside as the steering wheel melted into his palms. He looked through the windshield toward the mountains. A long, smooth stretch of desert rolled out before him, disappearing into a haze of distorted air. He imagined who had sat there before him, looking out across the great expanse. Why had he come out here? Was it a suicide? A crazy man? A drunk?

"So what do you think, James?"

"I don't know. We called the rental company and ran the driver's license they had. Guy from Chicago. Nothing came up. No history, no tickets. Nothing."

"And the purse?" Red asked

"Looks to be the wife's. Same last name on the ID, same address."

"Hmm."

"So a guy just decides to get a car one day, drive it out in the desert, and walk off?"

"Looks like it."

"I just don't get some folk," James said

"Yeah, sometimes it looks like the world's gone crazy."

Red started to get back out of the car. As he placed his foot on the ground, he noticed something. A skid mark in the dust in front of the back wheel, as if the car had been pushed back with the wheels locked. He knelt down to examine it closer. Putting his finger on the mark, he looked up at his deputy. "You ever see wind move a car?"

"I seen it on TV when they show the hurricanes and stuff."

"Yup." Red stood and scanned the horizon. The heat was starting to subside as evening came on, but it was still intolerable.

"What you thinking, Red?"

"Best call the boys in. I doubt they're going to find anything. And get a tow truck up here. I'm sure the rental place wants their car back."

"What you suppose happened?"

"They walked off west, I suppose. Why, is anyone's guess. In this heat they probably didn't make it too far." Red started walking back to his cruiser, James following a few steps behind. "Lonely way to go if you ask me, but like you said, you just don't get some folk."

"Shouldn't we go looking for them?" James asked.

"Car's been out here for a while. In this heat, *if* they walked off, most likely dead by now. I'll call Carl to get up in the chopper and do a sweep through here. But I doubt he'll have much luck either. If people don't want to be found, not much you can do about it."

"Guess you're right."

"Go on now, get the boys back home and buy 'em a beer on me."

"All right."

The blast from the air conditioner hit his face, sending a chill down Red's spine as he got into his police car. He looked at the scene—abandoned vehicle, windswept ground, vanishing people. It could be something out of *The X-Files*. He had seen it before where people got lost out in the desert, their bodies found baked in the sun, but this had a different feeling to it. Ominous. Creepy. Perhaps the occupants had been snatched up by aliens. There were plenty of people out in these parts who would assume that was the case, even swear their lives on it if they caught a whiff of the story. Red wasn't one of them. He lived more by what his eyes told him. No, more than likely these were just some nut jobs who walked off quietly to meet their Maker.

The wind kicked up and blew dust across his line of sight. A good gust, short and quick. The Mustang didn't flinch.

His gaze turned west toward the mountains looming on the

horizon. He felt like he was being watched, as if the rock shadows were observing the men walking through the brush back to their vehicles. *The desert can play tricks on the mind, that is for sure,* he thought. *You can't judge a man who let it get to him. Even if he wanders off to die.*

That night, Jack lay in bed unable to sleep. Laura had moved off the couch and now slept beside him. Though the bed was small, she only occupied a small sliver of space, a mile away from him. Periodically he could hear Boots move about the cabin, small shuffling sounds in the dark. It seemed like the guy never slept, but crept around in the night from room to porch and back again.

He wondered about this man living by himself out on the edges. Only a crazy man would. Isolated, alone. No stimulation for the mind. Either that or a man hiding from something. Some dark secret that he wished no one to see. Perhaps he kept that cemetery out back as a memento of all things evil. His past buried beneath the rock. Jack thought about it, but assumed that if he was a homicidal maniac, there would be slim pickings out here in the boondocks to fulfill his desire to kill. No, he was not of that sort, he thought. He was just a misfit. An outcast. Someone who could not hack it in normal life.

Jack thought about how he had gotten there, how he found himself lying in a stranger's bed, with his wife curled up next to him. Four days had passed since the highway, or so his wife had told him. They were due back home now. He should be walking into his office tomorrow morning and getting back to work. But instead he was out here. Wherever out here was.

The highway. He would close his eyes and he could see the stretch of road in his mind. The dotted center line unfurling in the distance. Total hopelessness. The waiting. He wasn't sure if he would ever lose that feeling whenever he would get back behind the wheel.

Do we get to the places in life by one choice? One grand stroke of decision that points us on our way? Or is it a series of small, inconsequential steps that go unnoticed until we look up and see that we are far away from anything we ever wanted? Jack thought back to renting the car, to buying the airline ticket, back to scheduling the vacation on his calendar. So many small steps to end up here.

Laura sighed and turned in her sleep. Jack looked over at his wife. Her slow steady breaths causing her rib cage to rise and fall under her folded arms. So close to him and yet a universe away.

They had been close once. Their marriage had started that way, but now they were distant. Two separate beings occupying the same small spaces. In his mind, he could picture snapshots of happiness, but he couldn't see the slow steps of detachment. Each little thing that accumulated through the years that now forced a wedge between them. He wished at times that there had been one sweeping moment of change. One moment that they could look at, isolate, define, work away. But there wasn't. There were a hundred small glances, short words, curt comments. Too many to recall and sift through.

Jack heard Boots's footsteps walk back across the floor, up to the door of the bedroom, and then back again. Maybe the old man would come crashing through the door with an axe in his hand. Maybe Jack would leap up and beat the life out of the old man, saving his wife from dismemberment, and saving the day. They would ride off on horseback, she with her arms around his waist, in love again with her brave hero.

Either that or he would be chopped to bits while Laura cowered in the corner waiting her turn, a look of shame on her face as she realized she had cast her lot with such a horrible protector.

He thought of her sleeping in the passenger seat of the rental car, slowly wasting away.

Jack rubbed this throat with his hand. It was still raw as he sat up and took a drink of water. The water had warmed up to room temperature, but he didn't feel like walking to the hand pump to get a fresh glass. The idea of meeting Boots in the dark didn't fill him so much with dread as abhorrence. Better to sit back and be content with warm water.

He fought for sleep and won no prize. The back of his eyelids danced with the image of the highway. The heat rising.

The foreboding.

The blackness.

The shadows taking shape and racing toward him. *It makes no sense*, he said to himself as he thought about this last memory. The evil wind, racing down the highway toward the car, wrapping around him like a blanket and constricting his bones. No, better to rationalize it out of existence as the last throws of an overheated brain.

Hallucination.

Heat exhaustion.

The firing off of synaptic nerves before they went silent.

But it was the feeling he could not escape. The feeling that sat in his soul, accompanying the dark shades of psychosis. The feeling in the pit of his stomach of absolute loneliness. Absolute isolation from all things.

Soon, sleep did overtake Jack, and as an unknown blessing to him, he dreamt of nothing.

The next morning Jack followed Laura out of the bedroom and Boots met them standing in the kitchen.

"Yous feeling better this morning?"

"Yeah, I think so," Jack said.

"Well, all right then. You can come with me and help me get some grub."

Jack looked at Laura quizzically as he started after the old man, who was already out the door. "I should get something to eat first."

"I got some here for you," Boots replied, tapping a bag slumped over his shoulder. "And there be some breakfast on the table for you, Laura."

"All right," she answered. "You two have fun."

What a way to wake up, Jack thought. Not only was he following behind Grizzly Adams, but he got sent off by low-budget sarcasm.

Out on the porch, Boots grabbed a shotgun that was leaning next to a stool and slung it over his shoulder. "Let's go."

Walking west into the desert, five steps behind Boots, Jack watched the swaying of the gun barrel over the old man's shoulder. The rhythm of the walk mixed with the intensity of the shotgun drove any remnants of the sleep hangover out of Jack's head.

He had figured last night in the dark that he could take Boots if the old man charged him with an axe. A shotgun changed the equation. They walked on, with the sun at their back and their shadows shortening with each step. The western hills loomed large, but unapproachable.

"You ever kill anything, Jack?"

"What's that?"

"Kill anything . . . you ever kill anything before?"

"No."

Boots stopped and turned. "Came pretty close though, didn't you?" The chew in the old man's mouth dripped from his lip onto his beard as an evil grin stretched across his face. He wiped his arm across his mouth and the smirk was gone.

Jack's eyes lowered to the dirt at his feet. Boots turned and kept walking.

"Really ain't that hard. Just point at what you want dead, and bam!"

"That easy, huh?"

"Yeah, that easy."

They walked on for half an hour in silence.

Boots spit on the ground as he stopped. They came up to a small gulley that ran perpendicular to their path. Jack could see a worn foot trail that led to the bottom of the dried-up creek bed, and he followed Boots slowly down the ridge. To the north end of the crevice was a small patch of foliage, and Boots sat there staring at it.

"Why don't you walk down there and scare up some birds, Jack."

"W-w-what?"

"Flush 'em out, and I'll kill 'em quick."

Jack looked north up the creek bed, at the shrubs about fifty yards ahead. He couldn't process what was being asked of him. "You w-want me to walk down there?"

"Ain't hard, Jack. Just walk down there and they'll get spooked, fly up, and bam."

The idea of walking with his back to a crazy man with a shotgun did not sit well. Arguing with a man with a shotgun wasn't a good idea either. Jack slowly started walking backward with his eyes glued on Boots, and the gun.

"Come on, Jack, what you think I'm going to do? Shoot you?"

Jack suppressed the stutter that was inching toward his lips. "The thought crossed my mind."

"Naw. If I wanted you dead, I'd not bother with you in the first place. Sure ain't going to waste a shell on you."

Jack backed up a couple more steps, moving slowly down the creek bed. "I guess that makes sense."

"Sure does . . . you just have to trust me. Now turn around and get down there. It's going to get real hot here if we stand around all day."

Turning, Jack felt the sweat begin to leak out of every pore of his body. He forced his legs to move, as the exhaustion of the past several days mixed with the fear in his mind. One step, then another, looking at the ground for snakes and bugs, imagining Boots behind him with the gun trained on his back. With each step, he was sure he would hear a blast, then the punch of lead ripping between his shoulder blades. It seemed logical, a perfect place to off someone, down below the desert floor, out of sight of any living creature. Another step. He looked up and still saw his destination as if through a tunnel. The rock walls terminating in a small patch of brown and green. A cozy spot to die. Another step.

Suddenly he heard commotion ahead. Screeching and chirping, a covey of quail shot out of the shrubbery and raced up over his head. He dropped down as he heard the shotgun go off behind him. A second blast soon followed.

Lying on the rock, Jack heard footsteps approach. He sprung to his feet and checked his body manically for bullet holes and open wounds. There were none. As his pulse slowed back to normal, Jack watched as Boots picked up two birds off the valley floor and walked over to him.

"Good job, Jack. This should do us."

Jack stared back at Boots, panic and anger filling his body.

"You should see yourself. About jumped out of your skin. Haha, you thought I was really going to shoot you, didn't you?"

"No."

"Sure did. Let me tell you something. If I was ever going to do that, I'll do it to your face. Deal?"

Jack continued to brush himself off, trying to rub some manliness into his composure.

"Let's be going . . . getting a bit hot out here."

The day wore on in slow motion. They ate lunch together from the two birds. Boots was a master of the iron skillet, and all were full. They sat on the front porch and made small talk, as much as creatures from different worlds could.

Jack was disengaged. He felt unsettled. He did not want to be here. He wanted to get back. How could they have ended up in the one place on earth where a simple phone call to get them back to the city was impossible? It was simple—this old man was lonely, talking to his horse and dead people all these years and now had a captive audience. He wasn't going to let them go until he told them all of his stories of panhandling and skinning 'coons.

Laura was enthralled by Boots. She listened to his tales of desert life and the way things used to be. She seemed to be oblivious to the real situation they were in. She was still on a vacation of sorts.

Why was she encouraging this? Why was she not on his side? Why did she not back him up at times like these? Why couldn't she see that their situation did not improve from when they were sitting on the highway baking in the sun?

Boots talked about how he moved out in the old times. "Pushed out," he said, as if there was ever a place where he fit in. "Just not into what people got into." So he moved out here in the middle of nowhere. *His form of running away*, Jack surmised.

"Desert is a fine spot," Boots went on. "You can see a man coming for miles. Ain't no one can sneak up on you. By the time they get to you, they be worn down. Not ready for no trouble. People in town, they get all worked up. Little man acting big, big man acting bigger. Naw, you can have all that. Out here ain't no one act tough who ain't gone in a day or two. There is a peace to that."

"And the view is unbelievable," Laura said, looking out onto the western mountain range.

"Yeah, you can't beat that. Beauty and death out here. Up there on one of them mountains some plane fell out of the sky. Had some lovely lady from film on it. Don't think they felt much. Over right quick, from what I hear. Mountain probably didn't look too good from their eyes." Boots chuckled. He leaned forward in his chair and spit, tobacco turning the sand a deep brown before drying up and cracking again. "I've been up there a few times. You can still see some pieces of the plane. Must've been quite the mess."

"I can't imagine."

"It be a funny thing. You get up one day and then it ends. You don't see it coming, but you think you have all the time. That lady probably thought she'd make some more movies, live grandly. But boom, done." Another spit into the sand punctuated the statement. "Kinda like you, huh?"

"I guess you're right. I never thought we'd be here right now," Laura said softly.

Jack just sat listening, stewing in his recollection of the highway. Of his mistake. Of his failure. He was sure Laura's comment was aimed at him. A small dagger from a quiet victim.

"Bet she never thought she'd be painted across no mountain, huh? But it happens. Ain't nothing to do about it. It just happens."

"You sure you didn't drag them all back here and bury them, Boots?" Jack said, horrifying Laura in the process. *Good,* he thought. *Get mad. Wake up!*

"Naw, Jack. That would be a long haul from up there." Boots spat again, seeming not to notice Jack's tone.

Jack got up and paced the porch before walking off around the house. He just couldn't sit any longer.

"A bit antsy, that one."

"Yeah"—Laura smiled—"he gets anxious pretty quick."

"I've seen it before. Man who can't sit down ain't never happy. Always got to be going somewhere."

"He's a good guy, Boots."

"You say so. Man like that get beat down mighty quick where I come from."

"He just wants to get home. We both do."

"I can understand that. You seem to be taking it all good."

"Yeah, I'm kind of enjoying this. Like I said, I never thought I would be sitting here right now."

"Never can tell what'll happen. You get home, don't worry. Just be patient."

"Okay."

"I can take *you* out, if you want. Jack don't seem to care about it."

"Oh no, I couldn't imagine leaving him here, or rather, having to have you deal with him alone." She smiled, and Boots smiled back.

He pulled the plug out of his cheek and refreshed it with some fresh chew. "Yeah, he's an ornery cuss. If I'm here by myself with him, I'm liable to put him in the ground out back."

Red sat behind his desk and thumbed through some paperwork. Not much had come down the wire. A few funny stories from the next county, but another light day here in nowhere. He had a rough night's sleep, never able to fully settle down, and it wore on his face today. Officer PJ was sitting in the other chair directly below the oscillating fan, which caused her blonde hair to blow every which way. Red found himself peeking at her out of his peripherals and laughed to himself. Yeah, he was old, but he wasn't dead yet. It finally got the better of him.

"Can you move, for Pete's sake?" he said with a grin.

"Oh, sorry, Red, am I blocking the air?"

"Yeah, exactly."

"Sorry about that."

"Thanks."

PJ moved her chair closer to Red's desk and took a good look at his tired mug. "You're not sleeping good?"

"Not so much last night. Kept thinking about that car out there James and I looked over yesterday. It just didn't seem right."

"What you mean?"

"Well, you get a couple, pretty well off from a big city. They come out here for a couple days, stay at a pretty fancy place. One day they rent a car, drive it as far from any living soul as you can get . . . get out . . . walk off . . . and disappear."

"Two of them?"

"Rental and hotel clerks said they were husband and wife."

"Murder-suicide?"

"Could be. No blood in the car though. That's a long way to go if one of the people don't want to go, you know? I would assume they both drove out there on their own accord."

"Robbery, then double homicide?" she asked as if chomping at the bit.

"Purse left in the car with a string of credit cards. Seems like that would be gone if it was a robbery."

"Mob hit?"

"You watch too much TV." Red chuckled. He liked the banter, no matter how ridiculous. It made him feel young, less lonely. "No, there was just something strange about the whole scene. It was like that car hit something out there. Something that stopped it cold."

"A rock?"

"No, almost like a wall or force field or something. I don't want to sound crazy, and maybe it's too late for that, but . . . it looked like the air just pushed it back and kept it from moving. Makes no sense."

"Hmmm . . . aliens maybe?" PJ smiled. She gave a girlish wink to Red and he managed to keep from showing his embarrassment.

"That'd be something, wouldn't it? Make this easier to explain. Naw, probably something simpler, it's just my mind won't stop racing to the extreme, you know? Most likely scenario is like you said . . . murder-suicide. Probably one of them killed the other someplace else, and then drove out there to do themself in. That would be the most likely scenario."

"But you don't feel it? You don't think it's something *simple* like that?"

Red stared down at his desk in deep thought. There was a sensation like a small candle burning in the back of his skull, an idea slowly morphing but still not in a comprehensive form. He looked back at PJ, who waited with extreme interest, and shook his head.

"No. Something out there just didn't feel right. I don't know what it was, but I think this couple ran into something out there. What it was or who it was, I have no idea."

Jack stood by the back fence posts and stared off into the distance. Beyond the endless horizon, he wished in his gut to see a sign of humanity somewhere out there that he had missed. Something that he could point to, grab Laura by the hand, and start running toward. Some beacon of freedom. He thought of different prisoners in history, because that is how he viewed himself now.

A captive.

A hostage.

The only difference was that he was bound in by infinite space. Pinned down by an ever-expanding universe.

He envied the traditional prisoner to the degree that they could see their walls. To see the cinder block, the razor wire. At least then you could focus your mind. You would know where freedom was, just on the other side. But where was freedom out here? One step out changed nothing.

One of Jack's favorite stories was about a man who managed to escape the frozen prison camps of Siberia and walk thousands of miles to freedom in India. The narrator had trekked through mountains and deserts, snow and heat, all in the quest to be a free man. It was an inspirational story that every office jockey dreamed of having the cojones to attempt. The fact that the story was a fake had crushed his inner adventurer. Of course it was a fake, Jack thought as he scanned the rock sea in front of him; no one could survive this.

The horse snorted and woke Jack out of his daydream. He looked over at the mare, who stared back at him.

"What are you looking at?"

The mare just stared back, passive eyes boring a hole through Jack's head. He walked over to the horse but did not touch it.

"I bet you'd like to get out of here too, huh. Penned up in this forsaken place. What kind of life is that for you?"

With a constant flick of the tail, the beast swatted the flies off its back, and seemed to enjoy the conversation it was having with the man.

"I bet you'd like to run free, just get out of here and run."

The mare stamped its hoof, and then again. It kept stamping and now started to jump around the pen as if something Jack had said spooked the life out of it. Its neighing and clopping building louder and louder as the horse worked itself into hysteria. Jack stumbled back, wondering what he did to cause the animal to freak out.

He turned around, ready to start yelling for Boots, when he saw *them.*

He was wide awake.

This was no hallucination

They were real.

Like a low, pitch-black fog, a stream of shadows rushed north across the desert at the base of the western mountains. Its origin stretched south beyond imagination. A raging river of wind and dust moving faster and faster like a midnight freight train. The horse went crazy, stomping, jumping, snorting.

"Boots!" Jack screamed. He screamed again as sand started blowing across his face, the clear air moving with the black rip current, a sandstorm building. The old man came running around the house. He went straight to the pen and calmed the horse, leading it into the little shed and shutting the door. The wind intensified, blowing harder and obscuring the blue sky above.

"Get inside, Jack! Move it!"

Jack ran to the front of the trailer and through the front door. Laura was standing in the kitchen, a look of worry across her face as the wind increased in intensity outside.

"Where's Boots?"

"He was right behind me!"

Jack ran to the bedroom and looked out the window onto the back. He could see the horse shed through the blowing dust. The horse tucked away from the wind but probably going spastic locked away. He could see the mountains, with a black band of swirling shadow at the base. It was pulsing, moving faster and faster, whipped into frenzy. All this he saw, his eyes wide open, his head clear.

Out by a fence post, Boots stood erect in the wind, staring at the mountains. He seemed unaffected by the haboob brewing around him. His beard flapping in the wind, filling with dust. Jack pounded on the glass, but the old man didn't turn. Laura came up behind Jack and looked out the window too.

"What's he doing out there?" she asked.

"I don't know."

"We need to go get him."

"We need to stay in."

"Is he crazy?"

"I don't know."

They watched as Boots raised his hand toward the west and started shaking his fist. His mouth was moving as if he was yelling at the wind. Scolding it, chastising an unruly class of hellions. He screamed and bellowed, but the sound of his voice barely penetrated the glass.

The black clouds slowed and the winds began to ease. They began to huddle at the base of the mountains, where their stillness caused them to disperse into nothingness. The blowing sand settling back to the ground and the blue sky reappearing overhead. Boots lowered his hand and turned. He walked back to the shed, opened the door, and led the mare out to its pen. He patted its neck, and then spanked its back end. The horse trotted out, shaking off its fears in the gravel and dust. Boots walked up to the trailer and noticed the couple staring at him through the window before they could duck out of sight.

"What was that all about?" Laura whispered to Jack, trying her best to understand what she thought she saw.

"I have no idea."

"Did you see what he did?"

"What do you think he did?"

"Stopped the storm . . . he stopped . . ."

"No, he didn't."

"But, Jack, he—"

"He didn't."

They heard him come in the front door, his boots clicking on the floor in the hall.

"You all can come out now. Storm's done."

They walked out of the bedroom cautiously, not able to hide their perplexed state of fear before the old man.

"Winds whip up pretty quick out here. No big deal."

"What were you doing out there, Boots?" Jack asked, point-blank.

"Having a bit of fun, I guess."

Laura looked at Boots, trying to figure out this puzzle of a man.

"Yeah, nothing like a good storm to wake you up."

"So you went out and yelled at the wind?"

"Haha . . . good a time as any to get some things off the mind."

Laura looked at Jack and back to Boots, her tension and confusion easing every minute. She couldn't explain what she thought she saw happen, but Boots's personality warmed her every time he started talking. No, she thought. He wasn't crazy. Maybe eccentric, odd, but not crazy.

"You yelled at the storm, and it stopped?" Jack asked.

"Now that don't make much sense, does it, Jack?"

Molly sat in the corner of the cave. She had lost track of the days. She would wake up, not realizing she'd been asleep, and drift back into dreaming. The absence of light messed with her inner clock. It could have been days, weeks. She had no idea.

Colten would come in, throw some provisions before her, light a cigarette, and watch her eat. Sometimes he would talk, sometimes he wouldn't. It was the times he wouldn't that worried her the most, as if any part of this nightmare caused less panic than others.

She looked up and saw him as he entered the cave and began the now habitual routine. He was silent, but his silence was more than an absence of speech. He was a black hole pulling in every sense of home that she had managed to maintain. Her stomach tightened and she pressed against the wall, the cold stone grinding her vertebrae, and wished the rock would embrace and hide her just as her mother's arms used to do when she was younger.

Colten had driven out there that day in a trance. Today was it. Today was the fruition of the week's game. The girl was broken. Yes, he had thought about it all day, sweating in the little convenience store. The excitement and anticipation had slowly built throughout the hours and would now climax in the final act. He stood against the wall of the cave and watched her eat the small bag of chips and wrapped sandwich that he had brought. It was pointless for her to eat. He knew that, but keeping her hoping that salvation would come was more important than the three dollars spent on wasted food.

His fury had followed him here, the wind whistling through the canyon. Darkness eroding a sunny day; his mood shape-shifting the atmosphere. He watched her chew, slowly savoring each bite. His rage building as he envisioned ripping her apart right then and there. Her screaming out for her mother with her last breath, a tear rolling down her cheek as the fading dream of home burned out of her eyes. His hands sweat with anticipation, his legs begging him to set them in motion, to bring him to her, to begin the process of erasing her.

Colten walked over to her and squatted down. Looking into her face, he began to channel every evil thought in his mind, every bad thing that had ever happened to him, and everything he ever wanted to say to his oppressors. The air began to stir, and the storm outside the cave increased with each passing thought. He reached out and grabbed her by the back of the neck. She screamed as his grip tightened.

But then, in the back of his mind, a glitch formed, like someone had pressed a thumb on an old bruise. Silent whispering sneaking up his spine, staying his rage, binding his resolve.

He looked at her, and loosened his grip on her neck. Once free, she cowered next to the wall, breathing heavy and consumed by shear panic.

"Naw . . . something ain't right. Not yet, at least."

The air outside began to settle, the storm held back by an unseen hand.

"Naw . . . you're not ready yet. Something . . . something just . . ."

He walked over to the other side of the cave and lit a cigarette. He leaned up against the wall, putting one leg back and resting one hand on the lifted knee. He stared at the girl, who was slowly untangling from her fetal position.

"Tomorrow . . . yeah, tomorrow would be better."

Colten flicked the cigarette across the cave, and it hit the rock next to the girl. He rubbed the back of his neck, a vain attempt to rub out the nagging feeling of doubt hung up in his spine.

"Yeah . . . it just ain't time."

He walked out to his truck and headed back down the mountain.

The girl's whimpers turned to sobs as the fading ember of the cigarette butt died in the darkness.

Having come back in from the storm, Boots appeared distracted, as if he was searching his thoughts for a vague recollection. He set about the cabin in silence, looking for items in a haphazard way and stuffing things into his satchel. Jack and Laura could not see exactly what he was grabbing, but both got the sense that the old man was preparing for a short journey. Finally, Jack broke the silence.

"What are you doing, Boots?"

"Just got something to get to."

"Are we taking off?"

"Naw, just me," Boots said.

"Come on, Boots, if you're going to town, we can keep up with you."

"Ain't going to town, Jack."

"Then where are you going?"

"Nowhere you need to know."

Jack looked over at Laura, who was sitting on the couch. She appeared as uneasy as he felt. "Come on, let us—"

"I said, *nowhere you need to know*. Now I want you two to sit tight, and stay inside. Ain't nothing out there for you right now."

"Boots—"

"I mean it!" Boots yelled, staring Jack down with a force that he had not witnessed up to this point from the old man. His mild temperament replaced with harsh determination. "Now I got something to get to, and I want you to stay here."

"All right, all right," Jack said as he sat down next to his wife.

The old man closed his satchel, adjusted his hat, and went out the front door. In moments they could hear the neighing of the horse as it rode off toward the mountains and the soon-fading sunset.

"What's going on, Jack?"

Jack's deflated ego weighed down his words. "I don't know."

Boots made his way to the mountains with the speed and grace of a snake through the dimming light of evening. The horse carried him on without hesitation. The beast knew that if there was ever a time to question and pull against its master, tonight was not the time to do it. The pair made their way up a path of their own making, guided by the stern eye of the old man at the reins. The horse did not misstep, and though they had never trekked this way before, it was as if the trail before them was outlined in lights and arrows.

Cresting a small ridge, Boots stopped the horse and got down. He walked forward several steps and crouched on the ground. He could see in the waning light the two-track leading up the mountain and stretching across the desert floor in the opposite direction. Tire tracks lay fresh in the sand. The way the dirt was kicked up the hill, he could see that they were made by a vehicle on the descent. He was alone on the mountain, but then again, he knew he wasn't entirely alone.

Boots led the horse on foot, and the mare seemed to enjoy the slower pace and lighter load. The two walked up the side of the two-track, the mountain walls embracing them with cold invitation.

Boots laid his hand on the cliff wall, feeling the radiant heat of the day licking his palm. He stood motionless, eyes shut as if taking the pulse of the world. This was the place. This chasm spiraling upward and inward.

They walked on as darkness moved in around them. Enveloping them with each step. The mare's head held low as it trotted behind Boots, content with him to take the lead. They trudged on into mystery until the two-track dead-ended in a small clearing surrounded by rock, which produced the effect of standing on the floor of a volcano. The mountain walls stretched up above him, ominously looking down with ageless coldness.

Boots dropped the reins and the horse stood still. He walked across the opening to the far side where he saw a small cave cut into the rock wall. Without missing a beat, he went inside and disappeared from view.

Colten drove through the desert back to Goodwell in a trance. He had brought himself to the brink of hysteria, but something had nudged him back. It wasn't a prick of conscience, but a nagging feeling that it just wasn't the right time, that something had to be done before he could fully relish in snuffing the life out of the girl.

The dirt kicked up behind the truck as he drove in silence, his elbow on the open window as his hand rubbed his chin. Thinking, exploring the scenario in his mind. He was so sure of the outcome throughout the day that he felt a sense of disappointment in himself. A sense that he had faltered. Why was he waiting, what could be added to the act that would make it any more welcoming tomorrow? It made no sense. It made perfect sense.

He pulled into the small town and up to the gas station. It was getting dark. The sunset over the now-distant mountain range spilling blood red over the desert valley. He parked the truck and let it idle as he sat there, contemplating the whole scene again in his mind.

Walking up to the girl, grabbing her neck, and feeling the smooth, unadulterated skin beneath his palm, her look of terror and the scream building in her lungs. Yes, everything had been perfect, he thought. He should have done it.

"You should have done it. You had the chance," said Seth, now sitting in the passenger seat.

Colten was not surprised to find him in the truck now. His gaze remained vacant as he stared out the front window. "Yeah, but something just didn't . . ."

"Didn't feel right? What do you know about feeling right?"

"It just wasn't the time."

"Sure it was. You just lost it."

"I didn't lose it."

Seth stared at Colten. Colten glared back. The two of them looked cut from the same cloth, just at different times in history. The older man's button-up shirt showed the fading of time, dark patches under the armpits brought on by a life in the desert heat. His pearl buttons caught the last light of day and sparkled.

"So what are you going to do? You just going to sit here and sulk?"

"No."

"Huh, looks to me like that's what you're doing."

Colten opened the truck door and stepped out, leaving the truck running. He walked up to the shack convenience store and went inside. The fan was off, and the stale air hung thick as he went back to the cooler. Seth was standing there waiting for him.

"Quit hiding in here."

"I'm not hiding," Colten said as he reached into the cooler and pulled out a drink.

"Looks like hiding to me."

"Would you get off my back? I told you, it just wasn't right. I'll get to it sure enough."

"All I'm saying is you can't let these things go too long. You'll get crazy, it'll get messy . . . sloppy."

"I know how to do this . . . you of all people should know that." Colten stared at the man, his hatred building again with each sip from the aluminum can. They stood in negative shades, dim reflections in the cooler's lighted glow. "If you know everything, what do you think I should do, huh?"

"I'd go back up there and get it done."

"Why tonight? Just as good doing it tomorrow."

"Naw, you was right in thinking that something wasn't right . . . I'd get back up there quick."

Colten took another slow swig from the can, and then wiped his forehead with his arm. "What are you saying?"

"I'm saying that somebody is messing with your prize."

"What?"

"Just saying."

"Saying what?"

"Saying that someone has caught on to your work and has decided to deal himself into the game."

"Who? Red? He don't know anything."

"No, not Red. Someone you wouldn't know."

"So why should I be worried?"

"'Cause he's heading up there right now . . . to the cave . . . to steal your girl."

Colten turned and ran toward the door. He scampered across the gravel, opened the door of the still running pickup truck, and slammed it into gear. Tearing out of the station, he cut a crazed figure against the twilight. Riding shotgun beside him was the man in the dark shirt and pearl buttons.

"It'll be all right, Cole. You'll get up there and do it quick."

"I should have done it before."

"Yeah, but you'll fix that mistake soon enough."

Colten felt a morbid panic rush through his guts. His mind was racing a thousand different directions that he tried to untangle. So much different than when he had made this trek earlier, driving slowly and savoring the expectation of vicious deeds soon to be realized. Now he raced through the night, as scared as a young boy when he realizes that his father is on to his lies.

"Who is this guy?"

"Just some old-timer meddling in things that don't concern him."

"You know him?"

"Yeah, I know him."

Colten's steel stare switched from the blacktop to Seth and back again. "You knew he was coming, didn't you. You knew it and didn't tell me!"

"This guy's been around a long time, Cole. He usually doesn't get involved. Huh, usually doesn't care about a thing. Takes the world to come apart for him to get moving."

"Why now?"

"Who knows? He can't be figured out," Seth said. "Just get up there before he takes off with her."

Down the highway he drove until he came to the two-track in the desert. He turned off the highway, and the man in the passenger seat dematerialized out of the truck cab and dispersed into the dusty backwash of the truck's exhaust.

The cave was still a ways off . . . and with all his panic, all his anxiety, all his fury, Colten willed himself to press faster through the desert night.

Boots made his way to the back of the cave without the aid of any light. Though he had not been there before, he moved like a dwarf through the dark tunnels of Moria. The entrance soon gave way to a small chamber that was dimly illuminated by a chasm in the roof where star and moonlight fought their way to the cave floor. Stepping inside, he surveyed the scene.

To his left, Boots found a small, half-burnt candle and picked it up. Out of his satchel, he grabbed a match and lit the wick. The small flame did little to cut the darkness, but he held it in front of him as he walked forward.

Across the small room, Boots saw the young girl lying on the ground. Her legs were brought up close and she hugged them with her arms. Her dark hair masked her face and she appeared to be sleeping. The light from the candle reflected off a thin chain that ran from her ankle to an anchor bolt in the wall behind her. A captive.

Boots approached softly and worked the chain. The clasp opened and he freed her from its bondage.

The motion caused her to wake with a scream. Molly, in a state of narcoleptic hysteria, swung at the man and knocked him upside the head, causing him to spill over from his squatted legs and tumble on the floor. She shot up and gave him a swift kick in the stomach.

She felt weak and realized that she had no power in her leg. The blow didn't seem to faze the man. She backed up against the wall, shaking like a trapped animal and ready to fight for survival.

Regaining his composure in the dark, the old man stood to his short height.

"It's all right now, I'm here to get you out," he said, his voice echoing off the stone walls while his hand rubbed his stomach.

"Stay away from me!"

"Now, I'm not going to hurt you . . . all right?"

"Get back!"

The man reached down and grabbed the candle. Took another match and relit it. He then raised the candle to his face. "I know I ain't much to look at, but I'm here to get you out. Now don't go kicking me no more."

Molly stared back at him. Her eyes darting from the cave entrance, to the old man before her, and then back. She was sizing him up, thinking whether she could outrun the bearded elf who stood before her.

"You can run out that door and be in the same awful mess, or you can come with me and we can get someplace safe."

She sorted out her options as best as she could, but the endless days of hopelessness had exhausted every ounce of energy she had. Just standing was proving too much to handle as her head began to swim. She fought the urge to faint, not wanting to be like one of those movie heroines who collapse at the worst possible time, but the room began to spin and she fell under her own weight.

From the entrance, a breeze began to blow, slowly stirring the placid air. The moist, cool air one breathes right before a storm.

Boots looked at the entrance and then back to the girl now collapsed before him.

"You're not going to make this easy, are you?"

35

They waited in the cabin that night, confused about what they had experienced in just the past couple of hours. The randomness of all the week's events, from the near death on the highway, to the eccentric desert nomad, to the seemingly unexplainable paranormal power the old man had over the afternoon's storm. All of it seemed too much to comprehend, to process into a single coherent narrative.

Laura sat on the couch between intermittent walks to the water pump, flipping through decades-old copies of defunct nature magazines. Jack was his usual restless self, pacing the room, staring out into the blackness of the desert.

"What do you think is going on?" he asked.

"What do you mean?"

"He won't let us leave."

"You're crazy."

"Really?"

"He's harmless. Who knows how far away we are from civilization."

"So."

"He knows more than we do about how to get out of here."

Jack could not accept that. He wasn't going to be bested by this old man. Not in Laura's eyes. "We should start out tomorrow."

"Where are we going to go, Jack?"

"There has to be someplace else. Something close by."

"We'll talk about it in the morning," she said.

"What?"

"In the morning."

"Hmph."

He paced on, always hoping that the next look out the window would bring salvation. He walked around the kitchen area, peeking into the three cupboards for anything that would resemble food. A late-night snack to ease his racing mind.

"Stop snooping around."

"I'm not snooping, I'm starving. This crazy old man has to have something to eat. He doesn't eat rocks, does he?"

Laura glared back at him. Late-night sarcasm never sat well with her. She watched as Jack paced the floor, first to the cupboards, then to the window, then back to the cupboards.

Nothing.

His stomach growled in anger, demanding its owner remedy the situation as quickly as possible. He kept searching and re-searching the area when what sounded like a sonic boom echoed through their bones. Dropping the magazine on the floor, Laura shot up, ran to the front door, and out onto the porch. Jack followed tentatively behind her.

To the west, over the mountains, they could see massive thunderheads against an otherwise clear sky. Another storm with twisting, churning motions like they had seen in the afternoon, but now at a distance that did not reach them. Where they stood, the air was still and calm. Up on the mountain, a vortex was unleashing its wrath on the stones and peaks. Black and gray swirling in a spiraling spectacle of Van Gogh's twisted mind.

"Wow!" was all Jack could muster. He had loved storms as a boy, what boy didn't? But this was of a magnitude he had never witnessed.

Laura stepped to his side and grabbed his arm, amazed at what she saw and a bit fearful at the same time. "Is that coming this way?"

"I don't think so. It doesn't look like it's moving at all. Just sitting up there."

"I wish Boots was here."

"Ha! I hope he's up there." Jack smirked. "The guy could use the bath."

Laura playfully slapped at him as a lightning bolt lit the sky. The crack took half a minute to reach them, but hit with an intensity as if it had struck the cabin. Her playfulness left her and she snuggled closer to Jack. They stood in silence watching Armageddon over the western sky.

In a breath, like black water sucked down a drain, the storm dissipated. Instantly. Unnaturally.

"Did you see that?"

"Uh, yeah . . ."

"What . . ."

"I don't know."

The silence strangled them. They felt exposed. Two souls in the middle of nowhere forced to huddle against each other for support and understanding.

"What is going on, Jack?"

"I have no idea."

The headlights of the pickup truck bounced off the rock walls as Colten sped up the mountain. His head swam with unrestrained rage. He had whipped himself back into a fury since leaving Goodwell, and now was in the state of mind he wanted to be. Dark shadows leapt from the paths of the halogen lights as they skirted across the jagged edge of the two-track. Faster and faster up to the cave.

He arrived at the clearing and slammed on the brakes, creating a cloud of dust that whipped up into the ever-growing wind. He was back. Now it was time to kill the girl. To complete the macabre waiting and move on. The slam of the truck door reverberated all around him as he strutted to the cave.

He had often thought of the taglines the villains used in film. There was the infamous "Here's Johnny!" that he thought was cool. Colten always thought he should make one for himself, a way of heightening the drama each time he stepped into this cave to do a kill. But he had never been creative that way. It would be imitation. He could never live with that. Besides, it was too much energy to devote to such a stupid thing.

No, he would enter the cave as he always did, silently. Without words, walk over to her, and kill her. That was the way he liked it. No explanation. No grand soliloquies. Quick and brutal and beautiful.

Colten stepped into the room and his blood boiled as he looked across the shadows and saw . . . nothing. He ran over to the far wall and felt for the chain. He found its empty clasp and threw it against the wall.

"No . . . NO!" he screamed as he ran around the small cave like a frat boy searching for a lost phone number. But it was pointless; the cave had no secret spaces, no hiding places. The girl was gone.

He ran out of the cave, back into the clearing where the chaos of the wind punched his face. His panicked eyes searching all over for her, around his truck, up the sheer walls of the mountain, down the two-track. She was not there. She had simply disappeared.

Suddenly the wind began to calm as Colten stood staring down the path he had come in on and out onto the desert floor several miles away. It was the only escape route. She had gotten out and now was trekking across no-man's-land. He heard a quiet laughing behind him but did not turn around.

"Should have done it earlier" Seth said, reveling in Colten's anguish.

"Shut up."

"What are you going to do?"

"Find her."

"You better. She knows what you look like. All she needs to do is tell."

"I know that."

"She can't get far—look at that," Seth said, pointing out across the wide expanse of the desert. "She'll probably die within a few miles of here."

"I need to find her."

"You will. But first, you need to collect yourself. Put your mind in order. Release some of this tension you've built up."

"Not now," Colten snapped.

"Yes, now. You're crazed! You're of no use in your condition."

Colten took a step back and turned to face the man behind him. "All right. What do you suggest?"

"Drive home. Get some sleep. Get something to eat. Start out early and find her."

Blood pumping through constricted veins. Pneumatic pulses in the eardrums prevented Colten from hearing Seth's directions.

"You listening to me? You need to focus."

Rage.

Uncontrolled.

Colten turned and made for his truck, got in, and tore down the mountain.

Boots kicked open the front door and rushed in, carrying the young girl in his arms. She looked like she was suffering the effects of a binge night, her emaciated face and sunken eyes, her body lifeless in Boots's arms. He walked passed Jack and Laura, who were sitting up at the table, and laid the girl on the old couch next to the wall.

"Great," Jack whispered to Laura, "he grabbed another one."

"Naw, Jack . . . I ain't *grabbed another one*, but the poor child is in a bad spot right now."

Laura went to the water pump, filled a glass, walked over to the couch, and started to wash the grime from the girl's face. Underneath the dirt, she was pretty. Maybe sixteen or seventeen, but with a little girl's face. Her clothes were a bit worn and several sizes too big for her frame. Laura moved the girl's dark hair from her forehead to reveal a large bruise.

"Did you do this, Boots?"

"Naw, she had that when I found her. Like I say, she was in a bad spot. Who knows what she'd end up with if I didn't show up. She'll be fine."

"You're a real hero, Boots." Jack's words dripped with sarcasm, but his expression wilted under the glare from Laura.

Ignoring Jack, Boots continued talking to Laura. "I found her just past the west ridge. Not sure what she was doing up there, but that was no place for her to end up. Bet she was dragged up there not knowing where she was going. Seen it before. Boys like to take runaways up there and have their way. Sometimes they leave 'em up there. Sometimes they don't. Yup, I've seen it before."

"Did you get caught up in the storm? It looked fierce."

"Storm? I ain't seen no storm."

Laura looked at Jack. He was sipping on his water, apparently disinterested in their conversation. She looked back at Boots.

"What storm?" she said, searching Boots's face. "The storm that was up on the mountain and then disappeared."

"Like I say, storms come up pretty quick out here, easy to miss if you ain't looking. I'll be sure to catch the next one. You take care of her."

And with that he scooted out the front door and was gone before Jack could respond.

Jack stood as the front door shut behind Boots. "Seriously? The guy vanishes, kidnaps a girl, drops her off here, then runs out? This is far beyond insane, Laura."

"Not now, Jack," Laura said, focusing her attention on the girl.

"Not now? Why not now? We are being held by some mountain man who is starting his own prison camp. Why doesn't he just let us go or lead us out of here? Why is he keeping us here?"

The girl began to groan and stir. Laura sat her up and held the water to her mouth. The girl sipped slowly at first, and then her eyes shot open, staring at Laura. The fear on her face was unmistakable. She pushed back into the couch as if she thought she could melt into the pillows.

"Who are you? Where am I?" she screamed, looking around the cabin for any sign of familiarity. Her eyes fell on Jack, who was now walking over. "Who are you?"

"It's okay, you're safe now. We won't hurt you." Laura offered the glass again with a motherly instinct and a faint smile. "What's your name?"

"Molly . . . ," she whispered. "Molly."

"Are you hurt, Molly?"

"My head hurts."

"You got a nasty bruise. Did someone hit you?"

Molly shook her head slightly. "I don't remember."

"How'd you get out here?" Jack piped in.

"I don't know," she whispered. "I don't know where here is."

"Good point. Somewhere in Nevada, I'm sure. Did some old man steal you from some place?"

"Jack!" Laura shouted.

"It's a fair question! She looks like she's been roughed up. She doesn't know where she is, and then Boots comes along and carries her in here?"

Molly pushed at the fog in her mind. Her body was past exhaustion, but she dug for memories while the couple argued on. They seemed all right to her. She felt no ill will toward her from them, just general concern, at least from the woman. The man looked agitated but harmless, like a small dog with all teeth but no bite.

"I was on my way to LA," she started slowly, scanning her mind through a cloudy haze. "I remember getting as far as Utah but then ran out of money. It was a lot more than I thought it would be." Molly took a sip of water. "I got a ride with someone down to Las Vegas. They dropped me off there and gave me a couple bucks. I was going to the bus station but didn't have nearly enough." Her mind searched for more detail, but that was where things became fuzzy for her.

"You remember anything else, honey?"

Searching her memory again, shifting folders around looking for some lost file. Her eyes darted from the floor to the wall, back to Laura's face.

"A truck . . . I remember a beat-up black truck."

Colten entered the bar well after midnight. He walked through the stuffy air to the back corner and sat down in an empty booth. He was sure that the dimly lit tavern would conceal his loathing. But he wasn't looking for a hiding place. He was out hunting, and this was the third venue of the night.

The waitress came over and asked if he wanted a drink.

"Draft."

He didn't plan on drinking it, but he knew that he couldn't sit empty-handed and go unnoticed. He wasn't sure how many more places he had to hit before he found what he was looking for. He had to keep his wits about him, and so when the waitress returned, he gave her a ten spot and called it good. He also had to be ready to move. Colten grabbed the beer and put it to his mouth, letting just a little quench his thirst, filtering a sip between his teeth.

He was off the Vegas strip. Away from the high-priced tourist spots but in a good locale. The frequenters of these places were either drunk locals or out-of-towners low on cash but still relishing the easy release that came from alcohol. His first two stops were a complete bust.

The first bar had been empty for well over a half hour. He felt uneasy. Exposed. He moved on before he was forced to make conversation with the bartender, who spent breaks between wiping the counter by watching the baseball game on TV.

The second pub had been occupied by a couple trying their best to crawl into each other's skin, and a small office party. The couple would not do tonight. He wasn't interested in twisting in a romantic vibe to his bloodlust. Tonight, he had a specific goal in mind. Bringing down to earth something big.

Now at a third bar, in the dark, moving the glass slowly in circles on the table, Colten thought about the day. He had planned to finish the girl off tonight. It would have been slow and calculated. He had waited almost a full week, relishing in the thought and planning every small detail. He had slowly worked her down to the bare, raw emotion. She would scream—of course she would—but she would scream for some pointed purpose, some focused stimuli, some single beam of pure channeled hope. He had learned when the kill came too quickly, a person's mind would scatter in ramblings, cursing, spitting. Messy.

Prepping her had channeled her suffering. At that moment when her last breath leaked out of her nostrils, he would know the one thing that kept her hope alive. She would scream it out. She would beg for it to help her, and be crushed when the full realization that that one hope would not save her. He would feed on the power then, the power of breaking the one thing that someone held dear. It was a better fix than the beer before him. It was better than anything.

But now she was gone before he'd had the chance to bathe in her misery.

Twenty minutes passed and Colten was about to move on when he saw *him*. The one who fit the night's order. The living corpse was sitting on the opposite side of the room, at the far end of the bar. Tucked in the shadows and blended with the wall sat a middle-aged bald man in a black T-shirt. He was big, several inches taller than Colten and at least 100 pounds heavier. The man's thick biceps flexed as he brought his cocktail to his lips and set the glass back on the table, the ice inside making an empty clink. There was a small, aged, unfinished tattoo peeking out from below the sleeve, an indication that the man wanted to be thought of as tough at one time, but had not wanted to return to the pain of the needle.

Colten didn't need a Rosetta stone to decipher his character. The shirt was too pressed and clean for him to be a real biker, and the redness of his skin confirmed that he was not used to the sun. No, this was some guy acting tough. Some guy playing the tough guy role. He could tell by the higher end liquor he had ordered to fill his glass. Yup, Colten thought, he would do just fine. It was not just sheer bulk that Colten had a desire to tear down tonight—no, he wanted to rip ego straight from the bone.

The man got up from the bar and paid his tab, then turned and walked out the door. Colten walked behind him and watched as the man jumped on a black VMAX and fired it up. Colten quickened his pace and got to his truck as the man shot westward toward the highway. It didn't take long for Colten to catch up and trail behind the unwitting soul.

They drove briskly out from Vegas north up the interstate until the darkness overcame the distant haze of the marquis lights behind them. Colten's face would glow as he lit the lighter and fired up another cigarette, his eyes on the single taillight of the motorcycle ahead of him. On the radio, the steady thumping of metal coiled his anxiousness around his spine. This was proving to be an adequate substitute.

For now.

The cat and mouse were the only two beings moving on earth at that moment, as if all other cars had vanished and they took center stage. All other souls asleep or watching in quiet, morbid fascination. The only lights on the road were the motorcycle ahead, the black pickup, and the occasional splash of a tossed-out cigarette butt. The motorcycle turned off the highway onto a county road before the lights of the air base lightened the night sky, and Colten moved in for the kill.

Accelerating to close the distance, he was on the bike before the rider knew what was coming. With a quick turn of the wheel he swerved into the rider and sent the bike skidding across the pavement, the rider eating stone and rock as he bounced down the shoulder. The man tumbled, his body becoming more lax with each punch of the pavement until he came to rest next to the hulk of metal that was his ride.

The red brake lights of the pickup truck illuminated the darkness, accentuated by the reverse lights as Colten backed up to the fallen rider. He put it in park, got out, and walked up to the man, who lay moaning on the road. Squatting down, he pulled the wallet out of the man's back pocket and looked through the contents, pulling out the driver's license.

"*David Wilcox.* Nice to meet you, Dave. Nice night, huh?"

The man lay on his back, trying to control the pain that was shooting through his body. He looked up at Colten.

"Says here you're from Minnesota. Long way from home, ain't you?"

"P . . . p . . . please—" the man was gasping—"call a . . . an am . . . bul—"

"Naw, ain't no need for that. Don't worry, it'll be over soon enough."

Colten walked over to his truck and reached into the bed. He pulled out two large chains and fixed them to his hitch. Then he strung one back and hooked it to the handlebars of the motorcycle. Taking the end of the other chain, he bent down and tied it around the waist of the fallen man.

"W . . . what are you . . . no please . . . not like this."

"Why not . . . got to be some way, don't it?"

Colten got into the truck amidst the screams of the man lying on the ground. He put it in drive and turned off the road into the desert. He felt a slight jerk as the slack from the chains abated and he slowly eased his tow off the road. Once on rock, he looked back through the rearview and saw the man wrestling with the chain.

Funny thing, thought Colten. The man knew what was coming, knew there was no way out of his fix, and yet still fought to prevent it. Colten didn't see the use but waited to gun the engine for a few seconds. An animal toying with its food.

Suddenly consumed by unmitigated rage and fueled by the pounding rhythm of the truck's soundtrack, Colten hit the gas and went plowing through the desert. The sound of scraping metal and flesh, screams of agony, and sparks of rock followed him as he drove on.

Faster and faster, swerving now and then to let the tow swing in arcs, rooster-tailing stone, spark, and blood behind him. He was crazed, like a heroin addict struggling to tie the tourniquet with shaky hands. He drove, dodging boulders and looking back as they reached up to punch both man and machine. After several minutes, he drove up to a dry creek bed. Colten hit the brakes and stepped out of the truck. He walked back to check on his quarry.

The machine was wrecked. The handle bars bent from the force of the dragging and the once-shining machine now triturated scrap. Small pieces of metal glinted in the dark, stretching behind them out of view. Colten reached down and unhooked the chain. He gathered it up and threw it into the back of the truck.

He walked around to the passenger door, opened it, and pulled a pair of gloves out of the console. He also grabbed a half-filled water bottle, shut the door, and walked back to the man. Or what was left of him.

There on the ground, unidentifiable to anyone who may have known him, lay Dave Wilcox of Minnesota. His limbs broken, contorted beyond repair. His clothes ripped and torn, pieces of fabric woven into the open wounds of his body. With slow, intermittent pushes, the man's rib cage would rise, forcing yet another breath into his pulverized body.

Colten squatted next to him and looked at the man's face. With all the energy he could muster, Dave Wilcox of Minnesota tried to speak, but only blood streaked down his torn cheek.

"Shhh . . . no use talkin'. Just let me enjoy this for a bit," Colten said as he took a swig of water.

"W . . . wh . . . why . . ."

"Ain't no use askin' why. It's done. Nothing you can do about it now."

The man looked up at the clear sky above him. Cloudless. Black. The streak of an airplane's exhaust high in the sky etched into his cornea as his rib cage fell and he died. Colten took another mouthful of water and spit it into the dead man's face.

He got up and removed the chain from the body, wrapped it up, and put it back in the truck. He got in the cab, turned down the radio, and slowly drove back to the county road.

It wasn't the grand night he had planned, the release he had hoped for since finding the girl at the diner, but it would have to do.

Only until he found her.

Hours before the dawn, Jack was awakened by the front door slamming shut and the sound of Boots walking across the porch. It took him awhile to realize where he was. Laura was in the bed with Molly, and he had taken the couch. His eyes adjusted to the darkness as he rolled off the cushion, moved to the window, and peered outside.

He watched as Boots stepped off the porch and strolled out into the light of a gibbous moon. Into the front yard where there was another man standing in the dust.

The man wore a black button-up with pearl buttons, an obnoxious silver belt buckle with the standard Wrangler jeans. His black hair was greased back. His cowboy boots appeared black under the layers of mud and dust caked to them.

Behind this mystery man there seemed to be a void in the horizon, as if cloud and shadow swept his footprints as he walked. Now he stood there, waiting for Boots to saunter up to the fence post where he was standing. Jack strained to hear them talk through the pane of glass.

"It's been awhile, Boots."

"I reckon it has."

"I can't believe you're still living out here. Place is a dump . . . but I guess that suits you."

"What do you want, Seth? I ain't got the patience for you right now," Boots said as he spat on the ground near the man's feet.

"Come on now, can't we just have a good ole heart-to-heart?"

"Speak. It's late and I'm tired."

"Word on the vine is that you're tinkering around again. Now, Boots, I thought we all had an arrangement that we were supposed to follow. We get to do what we want, and you stay out of the way."

"Naw, that ain't the way I see it."

"Hmm. Let me just tell you something. Things are a lot different than they used to be. I don't think you really have what it takes to step back in. So take my advice. You stay out here with your rocks and dust, and leave the world for us who know what to make of it."

Boots relaxed his shoulders and put his hands in his pockets. He chuckled and sneered back at Seth. "Ain't your place. You have a hard time rememb'ring that, don't you?"

"Where's the girl, Boots?"

"What's that?"

"Where's the girl?"

"What girl?"

"It's funny, you acting like you don't know anything."

"I know enough. I know your boy had no claim on her. Ain't had no claim on anything he's been doing."

"Suppose I send him down here to see if you ain't got her tucked away. He's real determined."

"You know how that would end . . . he'd be dead before he knew anything."

"You really had no business, Boots. That boy was just having a little fun. Now what is he supposed to do to pass the time? He gets cranky real fast these days."

"Ain't my concern."

"Nothing is ever your concern, old man. It's your excuse for everything."

"You come down here just to hear yourself talk?"

The man glared at Boots, then at the cabin, then back at the old man. "I see you got some company?" Seth said, licking his bottom lip as he stared up at the house and let his eyes settle on the window Jack was looking out of.

Jack swung himself back against the wall, a sudden chill running down his spine.

"I guess you can say that."

"Come on now, Boots, you can't lock people up against their will."

"I ain't lock no one up against their will."

"Really? From what I see, that man in the window doesn't want to be here at all. We saw what you did out there. That highway bit? Real nice. Ain't fair, but real nice. Make them waste out there for a while so they look at you as their savior. From the sounds of it, you almost left them out there too long. We almost took them in. You know, to help them out. Why don't I just go ask him if he wants to get out of this prison?"

Jack ducked back from the window again, his heart racing in his chest.

"He's doing just fine. I'm looking out for him. You don't need to worry." Boots spat again, but more out of attitude than necessity.

"Listen," the man said, straightening his spine. His hand still rested on the fence post, but the air behind him began to move in Edvard Munchian waves. "You can't keep him here if he doesn't want it. By all accounts you should kick him out. Them the rules. You going to go breaking the rules now? Huh?"

"Don't talk to me about no rules, Seth. What do you know about rules? You get what I give you."

The man growled, but he released his tension without saying a word. Mimicking Boots, he tucked his hands in his pockets, his shoulders relaxed, and the air stood still. "You're right, Boots. *I get what you give me.* And soon enough, you'll give me him. He doesn't belong here and you know it."

The man turned on his heels and started walking off into the night. He turned back to find Boots still standing firm, a small pool of spit forming on the ground in front of him and his hands still resting in his pockets.

"You're a has-been, Boots. Ain't no one want you around here no more. Pretty soon, you keep meddling, a world of hurt is going to come down on you."

"Maybe so, but I'm still here."

The man disappeared into the dark. The stars, which were unnoticeable before, began to shine brilliantly as if a curtain had been rolled back. Black cloth slipping from a tabletop.

Boots stood staring off into the night.

"I'm still here." His loud whisper carried to Jack's ear.

Boots stepped back into the cabin, slowly, like thick oil poured from a can.

"Who was that, Boots?"

"Him? Oh, you don't need to worry about him. As long as you're here, ain't nothing to concern yourself with."

"Nothing? Nothing?" Jack asked emphatically.

"That's what I said."

"He shows up in the middle of the night, asking about the girl and us, and you say it's nothing?"

"He's harmless, like I say, as long as you're with me."

Jack's stomach turned, his confusion, anger, and fear mixing toxically in his gut. "What did he mean by the highway?"

Boots was silent as he walked to fetch some water.

"Don't turn your back on me! What did he mean by leaving us out on the highway?"

Boots spun on his heels with fire in his eyes. "What do you want me to say, Jack? You looking for something to ease your mind about the way you drove yourself to the brink of dying? Take a good hard look at yourself. Deep. The way you been going, that road really seem like too much of a stretch? Totally didn't see that coming? Naw, you did that to yourself. You been doing that for a long time, from what I can see."

As quickly as the dagger was stuck into Jack's heart, the old man's mood shifted. His face eased and he looked sympathetically at the confused and broken man before him.

"It's late. You need to get some sleep. Now, don't worry about any of this. What's done is done. You're here now. That's all that matters. Tomorrow, things will look better. Promise."

The old man patted Jack on the shoulder, decided against the drink he had been going for, and went back outside to sit on the porch. Jack, left to himself, sat on the couch but didn't sleep.

The cycle was wearing on him. Mystery, anger, guilt. It always came back to guilt.

They spent the day keeping themselves busy about the cabin. The heat outside kept them in. Jack found it hard to sit still, his mind racing through the scene from the night before, trying to make sense of the scattered clues and words.

Laura was a quick nurse with Molly. The girl cleaned herself up and was walking around by midafternoon. She talked quietly as if worried to disturb the stillness of the cabin, and Laura did her best to coax some background out of her. She was a scared girl, like one lost in a busy store, searching for her mother. She was bruised up, to say the least, but did not look to have been violated in the worst way imaginable.

Her dark hair hung over her face as protection and accented her darker eyes. With a little white powder, she could have passed for any emo girl in any high school, but her features were natural.

"So why did you leave home?" Laura asked.

"Just felt like the right thing to do."

"Was it bad there?"

"Not really. Just bored, I guess."

Home was just outside of Columbus, Ohio. Molly suffered the fate of the typical teenage suburbanite. No matter how domesticated a young heart is, it still seeks a harder edge, not realizing how sharp that edge actually cuts. Usually realization comes after the carotid artery is nicked and there is little strength left to switch paths. For Molly, it appeared that she may have just missed that episode.

With slow recall, she began to recite the ordeal of the diner, the man in the black pickup truck, the cave. The utter hopelessness of the cave. She had no idea how many days it had been. She cried and Laura held her, and then she stopped and continued on, remembering the man coming into the dark with some food. How many times? She lost track.

She told of the madness in his eyes when she thought he was going to strangle her, how she prayed for her mother to come, prayed for anything to save her. Laura wiped the tears from Molly's face and listened quietly, her heart breaking for this child who had stepped out into a world she was not ready for. Laura would hold her when Molly needed it, and let her sit on her own when her strength returned.

For hours they shared the burden of the girl's misery until the weight of it no longer crushed her—the trick women have for surviving. Molly sat close to Laura through the morning and seemed to soak in the motherly attention she was receiving.

"I never thought it would end like this. I just wanted to get to LA, you know, see the big lights. Have a little fun. I just got tired of being a nobody in a nothing city."

"You made it a long way."

"I made it to the middle of nowhere, huh?"

Laura smiled back, secretly admiring the young girl's fearlessness in chasing a dream. "That's more than most people do. It took a lot of guts to come out this far. But you need to match it with a little smarts too. Does your mother know where you are?"

"I called her in Salt Lake City. She cried a lot on the phone. She was scared at first, then she was mad."

"Sounds about right."

"She told me to stay in Salt Lake and that she would come get me. I wish I would have done that."

"Well, there is nothing you can do about that now. Only thing that matters is what you are going to do next."

"I want to go home," Molly said, looking up at Jack, who had stopped pacing and seemed to have taken interest in the conversation. "I don't want this."

"That might be a good idea," Laura said, taking the girl's hand in hers.

"Yeah, assuming Boots lets you out of this shack of his," Jack blurted.

"Jack!"

"Just saying."

Molly pulled her hand back and stared at Laura, giving her that *Is he going to be all right?* look. "Yeah, I think that will be the best thing. Go back home."

"Good. We'll get this straightened out, I'm sure," Laura said.

The door opened and Boots walked in with lunch hanging from his fist. Some animal that had been kicking not more than an hour ago, now stripped of its skin and ready for the fire.

"Ah, good to see you gettin' around," he said, eyeing the girl. "I's goin' to gets this fixed and get some food in yous."

Boots made short work of the meal and the cabin filled with the aroma of wild game, panfried in a bit of oil. The three visitors could feel the grease hang in the air and coat them like a pungent lotion but did not complain, the hunger pangs in their stomach overriding any sense of ungratefulness. Soon the group sat down for a Spartan dinner of meat served with an unrecognizable side dish of unearthly greens.

Molly devoured her plate as if she had not eaten in weeks, and Laura generously offered some of her share, which the girl took without reservation. They ate in silence, each to their own thoughts.

After lunch Boots took leave out on the front porch to sit in his chair and chew. Jack followed after him stealthily, the memory of last night's scolding still weighing heavy on his mind. The image of the nighttime mystery man didn't sit too well on his heart either. A sense of impending doom lurked behind every thought. He needed to get out of there. To get home. To get back to normal 9-to-5 life, away from all this confusion and meaninglessness.

"So you think we will be able to leave soon?"

"You in such a hurry, huh? What's the matter, Jack? Getting sick of rabbit already?"

"Look, Boots, I'm grateful for what you've done for us—"

"Really?"

"—but we need to get back to our lives. I can't afford to stay out here longer than I have to."

"That's a funny way of putting it, Jack. How long could you have afforded to stay on that highway? Looked to me like you were getting ready to sit out there for a while."

Always with the guilt, Jack thought. Would he ever be able to live that down? Would he have to bear that mistake for the rest of his life? He could imagine himself back home in the grocery store with Laura, and her asking him what kind of cereal he wanted. He would say corn flakes, and she would respond with "Are you sure that's what you want? It would be a pity if you were dying on a highway and you suddenly wanted shredded wheat."

Any mistake Laura ever made would be a free pass. She could pay a bill late, stay out with friends all night, even have an affair with an old high school flame, and all she would have to say was "At least I didn't almost kill you!"

He would always have this burden. Even though he was sure Laura would not use it to beat him into a lap dog, he could not let it go. He was convinced that Boots sensed this and was using it to get under his skin.

"You got to loosen up, Jack. You'll get home soon enough. You think I enjoy you being here acting all uppity?"

"I guess not."

"You got that right. Why don't you go inside and leave me in peace. Unless you want to be civil."

"All right, Boots. Let's be civil."

"All right."

"Why do you live out here?"

"I told you, I'm just not into what people are into these days. Better to live out here in the open."

"Kind of sounds like running away or hiding, if you ask me."

"Is that being civil where you come from, Jack?" Boots spit. "You call it what you want, ain't no bother to me. People live reckless. Always after something they don't know they don't need. People get all crazy over not having. You can keep all that. Out here, you got to live smart."

Jack sat quietly, waiting to pounce on any weakness he could find.

"Let me tell you a story, Jack. I was up around Reno a few years back. Living okay, back before the world went crazy. I walked to the store one day and I see this man just whipping his boy on the sidewalk. Merciless. That boy must've broke in and tortured an old woman by the way that man was beating him. I was across the street watching him and saw people, just like you, Jack, walk by and not say a word. Just kept on walking, minding their own business.

"So I crossed the street and asked him 'What are you beating that boy for?' You know what he says to me? 'Ain't no worry of yours, mind your business.' Well, where I come from, grown man beatin' a child is my business. So I grab his hand and push him against the wall. The kid got up and just stared at me, not knowing what to do. I looked at his old man and what I saw wasn't right. There was blackness in his eyes, soulless. That man had nothingness swimming around his skull. The look would strip the fear off a rattlesnake's tail.

"Then you know what happened? That same kid starts kicking me in the leg. Starts screaming at me to let his pops go! I mean the same kid who was getting a mouthful of fist from his old man now starts trying to beat on me. I looked down and saw that same blackness in the kid's eyes. Same nothingness.

"So I let the old man go and kept walking down the street. The man throws the kid into a truck and they drive off.

"I never could understand. You go out of your way to help a soul, pull it up from the mud, and clean it off, then that same soul just spits back in your face. Ungrateful lot they are. Ain't no use even bothering sometimes.

"So what you make of that, Jack? Ain't nothing to be done for them, is what I reckon. A kind thing ain't mean nothing no more, does it?

"The Good Book says we are the salt of the earth. You know what salt does, Jack? It keeps a carcass from rotting. Problem is . . . it's already dead. So I figure, let 'em have each other. Ain't no use. Let 'em rot."

Jack stirred in his seat. He couldn't make out whether Boots was a coward or not. Was he a man of conviction making a silent protest, or was he a recluse who was overwhelmed by the real world? Was he a weak man intimidated by the toughness of life?

The things we hate in others are the things we hate about ourselves, Jack thought. He looked in the door and saw Laura chatting with Molly, and for a brief moment his heart softened and he saw Boots beyond his veil of cynicism.

"Well, it looks like you were able to help that kid in there."

"Yeah, but she'll go back to whatever she was doing before. She's got that wandering look about her . . ." Boots trailed off in thought, glancing off to the mountain and spitting slowly off the front porch. "Naw, girl like that need something a little more to push her back on the straight line."

"Boots, she was abducted and almost murdered!"

"Yeah, but she's fine now. Hopefully that'll scare her straight. I'll take her back to town in the morning . . . and she'll probably be back here before nightfall."

"Wait . . . you'll take her back tomorrow? Tomorrow?"

"What of it, Jack? You want to take her place? You want to leave your missus here and let me takes you instead?"

Jack stewed in his own silent rage, like a four-hundred-pound man who watched a little kid jump the line at an all-you-can-eat buffet. "No, that's not what I'm saying."

"It's what you're thinking though, huh? Like I said, Jack, you'll get home soon enough, but that girl in there needs to get back mores than you do. Don't she?"

The people on Jack's list of hate just increased by one as he thought of the hapless Molly who sat at the table talking to his wife. He knew it was wrong. This girl was alone and needed to get back home more than he did. But he couldn't help despising her. He looked at her as yet another thing that thwarted him from getting back to life. His resentment sprang forth from the same spring as his feelings for others who got in his way.

When he had first started out after school, he was stuck in line for promotion behind an old fart with seniority. The guy just wouldn't move, a manager who wouldn't retire and planned on working until he was a hundred years old. One day Jack went to work and found out the guy had a heart attack at dinner the night before and died. He mourned over the death for the obligatory five minutes and then started packing his desk as he prepared to move into the now-vacant office and his new promotion. He didn't attend the funeral, even though the company had provided time off for the employees to pay their respect to the firm's dinosaur.

And now he looked at Molly much the same way. The girl he had just sympathized with now filled him with simmering contempt. Here was a little vagabond who chose to run away from home, taking his spot on the next train to freedom land. What justice could there be in this world?

His stomach knotted again on the emotional roller coaster.

Jack went to walk inside but stopped in the doorframe. He turned to Boots. "Why don't you ride off and get help? If you don't want to take us, fine, but at least go get us someone who'll help us."

Boots stood, pulled the plug out of his cheek, threw it on the ground, and stretched his back. Once he was all adjusted, he looked Jack in the eye.

"You got to start understanding, Jack. Ain't nobody comes out here no more. And I ain't in the business of going off and dragging 'em in. You're here because you almost drop dead on my front door. Ain't no one come looking for you, did they? Naw, you were left on your own to rot. That is, until I's found you. So you leave when you want, Jack. Front door is always wide open. Just open it up and walk out, if you think you know best." Boots reached into his shirt pocket and pulled out his tobacco. He stuffed it into his cheek, then spit on the ground. "If you don't want to do that, then you'll get out of here when I think you're ready to go."

The old man stepped off the porch and sauntered into the front yard as if admiring the day without a care in the world.

Jack walked into the trailer slow, dejected, and furious.

That afternoon he had made up his mind. Through the setting hours, Jack planned out the details in his head. He found a small container in the cabin that he filled with water from the pump. His only reservation was that it would not be cold by the time they would drink it. At dinner, he tucked some food away from the table when, though out of character, he offered to clean up. A prisoner hoarding his rations. Boots had said that the front door was wide open to him, but he was convinced the old man wouldn't lay out provisions for them, nor would he take kindly to Jack stealing his supplies for their trip.

In the bedroom as they prepared for sleep, he told Laura of his design. "We're leaving tomorrow."

"Is Boots taking us out?"

"No."

"What do you mean?"

"I mean we are leaving, on our own."

"No, Jack, we're not."

"I'm not staying here another day. We need to get out of here. We need to get home."

"You have no idea how to get out of here."

"Easy, we open the door and walk east."

Laura folded her arms and stood next to the wall, facing Jack. Her anger was beginning to rise. "No, Jack. We wait here until

Boots thinks we can make the walk. He knows what's best for us right now."

"He doesn't know squat, Laura! Listen to yourself! We are stuck in a trailer in the desert with a bearded half-wit who chews tobacco like it's bubble gum and can't speak a decent sentence to save his life. Then he finds a girl who was kidnapped by some crazy local and stuck in a cave. Oh . . . oh . . . oh . . . and let's not forget that he runs out into storms and yells at the wind. I mean, come on! You can't make this stuff up. It's like an episode of the *Twilight Zone* or something! And you just want to stand there and wait for him to magically take us home?" Jack's sarcasm was flowing full force at Laura.

"Jack, you need to stop right now."

"I won't stop. We are leaving."

"Don't say 'we.'"

Jack stood silent, the wind knocked out of him. Laura, the passive wife, standing up to him, was new. He stared at her, a person who was now foreign to him with just one stroke of a brush.

"I'm not leaving. If Boots says we can leave tomorrow, then I'll go, but until then, I am waiting here until he says so."

He remained silent and walked out of the room.

She could hear him open the door and step outside, though there was no place for him to go.

Laura got into bed and lay there, thinking about the vacuum of space between her and Jack. This trip that was planned to bridge the gap may have broken them for good. They were alienated from each other like no other time in their history. She pulled the covers over her though it was hot, and cried silently in the dark.

Jack entered the room awhile later and crawled into bed next to her, but they did not touch. A force field surrounded her and was impenetrable. The silence was suffocating, and with a gentle breath, he whispered, "I love you."

She played at being asleep and did not respond to his unspoken question.

PART THREE

THE DESERT

Jack got up quietly in the middle of the night. He hadn't allowed himself to sleep too soundly. He walked softly over to the small four-paned glass window and nudged it open. The heat from outside instantly enveloped his face as he stared out into the night. He crawled through the window and squatted on the desert floor, where he pulled on his shoes.

It seemed an overly elaborate escape plan, but with Molly sleeping on the couch and Boots lurking who knew where, the window was his best option. He had tested it earlier that day and was happy to find that it did not make a sound when opened. Quiet.

He stood up and looked back through the window at Laura sleeping in the bed. He felt a twinge in his heart with the thought of leaving her here, but she had voiced her opinion of his plan loud and clear. They were no longer a team. Whether or not that conclusion would last after he brought back help would have to play itself out. For now, he had to leave, whether she was on board or not.

Looking at the stars, he tried to recall any astronomy lessons he may have slept through and estimated to the best of his knowledge what way might be east. He didn't know why, but he was sure Vegas was that way. Careful not to make a sound, he stalked around the corner of the house and walked off.

The situation ran through his mind like a grocery store check-list. *It has to be around midnight, so six hours until daybreak. You have little water, so you have to make some miles before the heat gets unbearable,* he thought. *You have no idea where you are going, or how far it might be to see another soul. Awesome odds.*

Trotting off into the desert night, Jack established a steady pace. The moon was not full but still illuminated the rock and dust, which gave off an eerie glow of haunting subtlety. In his mind he could envision the rattlesnakes and scorpions watching his progress through the dark and licking their chops at what might possibly be a free lunch by noon. The crunching sounds of his own footfalls were all that he could hear as he progressed to a small rise east of the cabin. He stopped and looked back at the prison trailer.

It wasn't too late to go back, he thought. He could simply turn around and walk back through the front door, take off his shoes, and get back in bed with Laura. She would wake up and be none the wiser to his jailbreak, to the idea that he had left her.

No. He had made up his mind. Jack was marching home and getting help to save her. He wished that their parting words had been more loving, but if they had been, he would not be trekking off alone. She would be following him right now.

What was going on with her? Ever since their "capture," for that is how Jack had labeled it, she seemed resigned to staying, almost welcoming the confinement as a relief. Perhaps he didn't know her at all. He told her that they should go get help; she said that they didn't need help and that he was being delusional.

The slow breaking had brought him to this moment of staring back, of imagining her sleeping alone in a strange trailer in the middle of nowhere. Small steps of detachment.

Then there was Boots. "He saved us from roasting to death out on that highway," Laura had said.

"No, he brought us here for some other reason . . . and it ain't good."

The idea of the old man brought anger. Jack refused to entertain the belief that Boots knew what he was doing. *He* was the delusional one, sitting out here in the desert, paranoid of living among civilization. Hiding away in a shack, safe from all the boogeymen a senile mind could think of. What help could he provide? None. Boots didn't want to help them get out of there, he was looking for fellow cowards who would validate his withdrawal from the world, who would keep him company as he hid.

Jack thought briefly that they all deserved each other, sitting in the tin roof dump. Members of the spineless huddled masses. He was not of that ilk. He was going to make things happen. He was directing his path, and if no one was on board with it, then he was going alone.

He turned back east, took a sip of water from the container, and started walking again.

His thoughts drifted back to the highway . . . where it all started. That seemingly innocent drive out from the strip. The week out here in the desert seemed like a total nightmare. Who could have ever imagined this, he thought. Getting stranded, and then getting held hostage. What he wouldn't give for the hour-long commute to work, of walking in and sitting in front of his computer. No, he just had to drive into the boondocks for no reason at all. If there had been a wall close by, Jack would have punched it. He kept on walking.

The highway. That long two-lane of nothingness. But there really wasn't nothingness, was there. The highway. That was where Jack first saw them, dancing and wailing in the convection. Down the road, where the horizon dipped past sight he saw them, hundreds of them, shapes distorted by the distance and the heat, but there nonetheless. He told himself that it was just dehydration playing tricks on him, but something deeper than that gave him a more somber chill, like hundreds of eyes staring at him through the mist.

And then they had appeared again in the dust storm. An endless cloud of malice whipping up a desert maelstrom. He couldn't blame that on dehydration. No, they had been there, physically, absolutely. Daylight might bring them back again. Though the idea sent a chill up his spine, confronting an evil mist still seemed to be better than sitting idly by.

He scanned the horizon. The night was cloudless. No storms in any direction. Nothing creeping up on him from the skyline. His spine warmed again in the dark heat.

On and on he ran toward what his body told him was east. His watch hadn't worked for days, but he kept moving through the fatigue and the brush as he tried to calculate the distance he covered . . . always calculating. *Ten miles . . . maybe fifteen . . . gotta be close to that . . . gotta be close to something, anything.* He crested a small butte and was crushed. The desert stretched on for miles with no signs of life, and on the horizon he could see the first edge of sunlight breaking through like a crack in a child's closet door.

Jack marched on as the hours ticked by. His trot turning into a slog as the sweat poured down his face. He hated himself for being out of shape. But he'd never imagined that he would need to train for such an event as this. He would have, he told himself, had he only known. The temperature began to rise as the day fully unfolded.

Knowing that he could not beat the sun, Jack looked for a place to hide. Halfway down a ridge he found a cave with an opening twice his size. He stood at its mouth and peered in. What hungry things lived inside? He could envision snakes and coyotes looking out, whispering prayers of "Oh please just one more step" in the darkness.

That would be quick, the sun would be slow, he thought, playing with death in his mind. He stepped inside and felt a few degrees cooler instantly. His bravery was thinly veiled, and he managed only a few steps before it failed him and he sat down.

Jack was exhausted. His legs were screaming and released slow pinpricks of relief when his weight was removed. How far had he come? A long way, he told himself. A very long way.

He unwrapped a small piece of meat he had hidden away from the dinner table last night and savored it slowly. His water was almost gone, but he drank it without hesitation. Civilization had to be just over the next hill. This was America, no less—how far could you go without seeing a subdivision sprout up before your eyes? Las Vegas had to be close, it just had to be.

After his meal, he slumped back against the rocks and tried to sleep. He could feel imaginary creatures crawling on his clothes, and every time he almost succeeded in drifting off, he would jump with a start, check himself, settle down, and start the cycle over again.

Soon, though, his exhaustion took hold of him and he was gone to the world.

Laura sat on the porch, staring in disbelief into the wasteland of the Mojave. Her mind was blank as she was unable to piece together the thousand fragments that swam around inside her head. Molly sat close by but did not talk to her. She seemed to know the times it was best to be quiet, a rare trait for a teenager, and thus she held her tongue. Boots came walking across the front yard, kicking up dust with every step.

"I don't see him. He just didn't go for a stroll, it seems."

"You have to go after him, Boots. He doesn't know what he's doing out there," Laura whispered as she imagined Jack dying a myriad of different ways and hating herself for enjoying some of them.

Boots stood in his familiar pose, his cheek filled with his hobby. "Seems to me, Laura, that he doesn't want me coming after him. Seems he likes things his own way." He turned and spit behind him in deference to the ladies seated on the porch.

Molly's widened eyes bounced back and forth between the two of them.

"He'll die out there," Laura said.

"If that's the way he wants it."

"That's not what he wants. He probably thinks he is trying to help."

"You give him too much credit. Naw . . . he's gone to save himself. Left you here on your own. What kind of man does that? Not a good one, I say."

"Please, Boots?"

The old man removed his hat and wiped the sweat from his brow. He looked up at the sky and then back to the porch, pondering the situation. "It's getting hot out today. Probably fry him up real quick."

Molly and Laura stared back at the old man, surprised that such easy talk could come in such a dire situation.

"All right, I'll go get him. But not right now. Naw . . . I think a man like that deserves to stew a bit. Make him think about what he's done."

"But—" Laura began, but was cut off by a wave of Boots's hand.

"That'll be the end of that. Now . . . you don't worry about him. I'll get him back."

He ambled off behind the cabin as if out for a morning walk, leaving the two women sitting on the porch.

Molly moved her rickety chair a little closer to Laura in a small attempt to offer comfort. "I'm sure he'll be all right."

Laura didn't answer, but looked down as a tear dropped from her cheek.

"Jack seems like a strong guy. I'm sure he can take care of himself."

"That's one thing he's good at . . . taking care of himself." Laura tossed a sideways glance at Molly. "He's perfected that art for many years."

Molly sat back, watching her, a patient look on her young face.

Laura rubbed her legs and sat up a little straighter, preparing to recite the script that she had worked on for a long time. The great venting. "Jack is very good at that. Always has been. When he gets something in his head, he can be a very determined man. It's why he is successful. Very determined. I used to think that he did things for me. You know? Worked hard for me, to show me that I was important. Now I know he just did things for himself. To make himself feel important. I just caught the spillover.

"There was this time . . . I can't believe I'm telling you this . . ."

"Go ahead."

Laura looked at the young girl and saw innocent concern in her eyes.

". . . there was this time when Jack came home with some news. He said that he got a promotion. A lot of money, a nice title. I was excited for him. He told me that the job was in Atlanta."

She started picking at the fabric in her shorts as a nervous release.

"I told him that was too bad. I still can't believe I said that to him . . . but it felt good. I told Jack that I wasn't going to move to Atlanta. He spent about ten minutes trying to tell me why this was a good opportunity for us. I told him that he would have to take the job without me, because I was staying.

"He got pretty mad and left. A couple hours later, he came back and said that he had decided to pass on the job."

"Well, that seems like a good thing," Molly said.

"It does, doesn't it? He thought so. He still feels like he sacrificed for me. But you know something. It took him three hours to decide. Three hours to weigh the choice and the consequence. He didn't take the job because he felt guilty, not because he wanted me to be happy too. He just didn't want to show how selfish he could be.

"It's why we came out here. Out to Las Vegas. Not just that, but this whole charade we've been living. I thought this would be good for us. To get away. Rekindle something. Start fresh. Huh, no. Even out here he's found a way to . . . found a way to be . . . himself."

Laura drifted off into her own world again as she stared toward the horizon. In her mind's eye she could see the silhouette of Jack walking through desert brush, tripping from exhaustion, lost and too proud for help.

Molly ventured to take Laura's hand and she consented.

"You are a strong woman, Laura," the girl said. "You have a good heart. You deserve to be happy."

Laura smiled at Molly's attempt to sound older than her youth allowed. She didn't want to break the bubble of adolescent optimism by letting her know that "deserving" had nothing to do with it.

The black pickup truck drove through the noonday sun, Colten sweating with manic frustration. The killing the night before had calmed his nerves, but he had worked himself up again. He had to find the girl. His thought processes were not working properly. He would never have been as reckless as he was with the biker if she had not taken off. No. He had to find her. Zigzagging through the shrub and stone, he kept his eyes peeled for any movement, but he found none. His bloodlust whipped up to a frenzy as the beats and suspension pounded his heart rate.

"You have to find her," Seth said.

"I know."

"If she gets to someone, you're done."

"I said I know!" Colten screamed.

He punched the gas as he swung back on the pavement from the desert two-track, a cloud of dust behind him that instantly flashed red and blue. A police cruiser coming up the road behind him.

"You think they found the girl?" Seth said with a faint grin.

"No."

"You think the girl told them?"

"No."

"I bet she did," the man said with a curt smile.

"Just shut up!"

Officer PJ Morey stopped her police cruiser on the side of the road behind the black pickup truck. She could see the heat rising from the roadway as she put the car in park and dialed up the radio. The thought of getting out of the car was not on the top of her "most favorite things to do" list, but this was her job, and she took pride in doing it well. The voice on the other end of the radio sparked up, and she got to work.

"Yeah, Red, I need you to run a plate for me."

"What's you got, PJ?"

"Black pickup out driving crazy."

"Slow day. Hold on a bit."

She put the radio down and waited for a response. Looking out across the road, she thought about being at home. Such a nice day, it would be better to be poolside with a cold drink than passing out tickets. And poolside is where she belonged, according to many of the hometown folks. But she was out here, being a cop despite all the concerns and naysaying of her pops. Many had placed bets that she would have had a hundred kids by the time she was twenty-five, but she pushed that life aside as soon as she was out of high school, enrolled in the academy, and went to work. It wasn't her *whole* life. She knew that, and she daydreamed of lounging around in the heat as any right-thinking person would.

Officer Morey didn't graduate at the top of her class, but she had learned all the skills of being a good cop. Plus, countless episodes of *CSI* had filled in the gaps.

She kept an eye on the black pickup, making sure the lone occupant wasn't busy stashing stuff away in the cabin. She had heard stories of big drug busts out on the stretches of highway in the southwest, but nothing like that ever happened around here. She had to read about such stories back at the station.

Just this morning she heard about the body of a man found outside the air base north of Vegas. The guy was found off the highway, seemingly dragged to death across the desert floor. His bike was next to him, twisted and broken. It too looking as if it had been dragged, pieces of it found strewn in its wake. The bike had Minnesota plates. Tire tracks leading out of the desert were waiting to be analyzed. Brutal and interesting. A killer on the loose and officers up there racing to find him. Or her. No, no cases like that down here, she thought, just boring routine and heat. She came out of her daydream when the radio came back to life.

"It's just Cole, PJ. Better go up and make sure the boy hasn't been drinking, then turn him loose."

"All right."

She opened the door and stepped out of the car.

Colten watched the officer in the cruiser from his rearview mirror, the sweat in his palms greasing the steering wheel as his knuckles cracked from their grip. He watched as the blonde-haired cop pulled the radio to her mouth and put it down again. She sat there waiting, waiting for him to make a move, it seemed. An eternity later she voiced something back in the radio and stepped out of the car.

"So, this is how it ends, huh?" Seth said.

"No, it's not."

"She knows. That person on the radio just told her. You're done."

"They don't know anything."

He watched as the petite cop walked in front of the cruiser and toward the passenger side of the truck.

"Good luck."

"Just shut up," Colten replied, but the seat was empty. Just the silence of his own thoughts and the idling engine accompanied him.

PJ walked up the shoulder on the passenger side of the truck. She had read of officers getting struck by passing cars when standing on the driver's side, so she began to make it a habit of talking to speeders from this vantage point. Plus she told herself it offered her better visibility and protection if someone flew off the handle. The most it had ever done was save her from getting puked on by guys who had had too much to drink. The exhaust pipe shot a rank plume of smoke into her face, making her light-headed for a moment.

Getting to the window, she went to the formalities. "Driver's license and registration?"

Colten grabbed some papers from his visor and handed them to PJ. She took them with a nod and started heading back to the cruiser.

She thumbed the paper open and glanced at it, then flipped over the license. David Wilcox, St. Paul, Minnesota. She stopped in her tracks, a knot the size of a basketball welling up in her stomach. She looked up toward her cruiser and in her peripheral glanced at the back quarter panel of the truck. There were fresh scrapes that had not started to rust. New.

She forced her legs to take a few more steps, hoping that her hesitation had not alerted the driver.

Colten watched in the passenger side mirror as the cop walked back, examining what he had handed her.

Just get this done with, he thought.

His heart thumped in his chest. He had been reckless. Unordered. He knew that last night he had been twice impulsive, and this had allowed cracks to form. He should have killed the girl when he had intended, and then he never would have gone on a binge with the biker from Minnesota.

He saw the skinned face of the man in his mind, lying on the ground, looking up at him laughing. But why was he laughing now? No, that's not how it happened. He had died, begging for reason. Colten shut his eyes and shook off the vision in his head. Again, the laughing dead man in his thoughts. He opened his eyes and looked at the dash. Sitting there next to the ashtray was his driver's license.

A cold hand gripped his spine as laughter echoed in his mind. He looked back to notice the cop walking slowly around the back of his truck.

"She knows," said the laughing voice.

His heart panicked.

"Hahaha . . . SHE KNOWS!"

PJ stepped behind the truck and looked over the tailgate into the bed. On the floor she could see chains scattered about. Thick ones. Chains able to tow a vehicle . . . or drag a bike and rider cross-country. Her pulse beat faster as she put all the pieces together. Her eyes trailing the chains as they skirted the truck bed up toward the cabin. Then her eyes met his as he was turned, looking back through the rear window. They were soulless . . . evil.

The pickup truck slammed into reverse and she caught the tailgate with her chest, her arms thrown over the top with her feet dragging on the ground. It only took a second to slam into the cruiser, her body smashing through the radiator. She felt nothing as her back broke. She could not breathe but short gasps as she lay pinned on the hood of the crushed police car, staring upward. The sweeps of clouds spun in circles.

Her head rolled to the side and she could see the ground under the driver's side of the pickup. Her mind struggled to process this as her body went into shock. She could see Colten step out of the truck and walk over to her. He reached for her hand and pulled the driver's license from her clenched fist. Then stood back and stared at her.

"It's a shame. Could have been anywhere today. Just so happens you were here."

She cried a faint tear as the thoughts of an unlived life passed before her eyes.

"Now I'm going to do you a favor. I'm going to move the truck and you going to die real quick. But since I wasn't planning on any of this, you tell me when."

Officer PJ's mind spun with the clouds overhead as she thought of the morning, of the desert, of her family, of all the things in life she had done and would never do. She felt calm. Not so much at peace, but slowly processing the facts. She was already dead. Her body just didn't know it yet.

She rolled her eyes up to Colten. Not able to speak . . . she simply nodded with her eyes.

He turned and got into the truck, put it into gear, and rolled forward. The cop's body fell with the pressure released, and Officer PJ was dead before her head hit the ground. Colten put the car in park, got out again, and surveyed the scene. His companion returned.

"You are just out of control now, aren't you?"

"I had no choice. She knew."

"She knew because you as much as told her."

"I know."

"You know you're done now, right?"

"I know," Colten said.

"Come on, let's get going."

Colten got back in the truck.

There was no use trying to cover up the mess. The cop had obviously called in his plates. They knew where to find her, what she was doing, who she had stopped. The man was right. He *was* done. They would know everything soon enough. They would be after him.

"They are going to put you in that cell. And all you'll have to think about is what that injection will feel like."

"Shut up . . . let me think!"

"It's going to be a long wait."

Colten put his head on the steering wheel, rocking back and forth, trying to clear his mind.

"You know what will help pass the time? Remembering that girl. Yes . . . a memory like that will last a long time. She's still out there. Ain't nobody important found her yet."

A silence filled the truck as it started to ease down the highway.

"Let's go find her."

Sitting at the table, staring outside, Laura sensed more than saw Molly walk back to the couch after fetching another glass of water from the pump and plop down on the tattered cushions. She felt the girl looking at her but kept her eyes on Boots, relaxed on the front porch.

Her thoughts were on Jack, wherever he might be. The heat from outside was unbearable, hotter than any day so far. He was an indoor creature, she knew, and the temperature would make short work of him.

After a while Laura walked out to Boots and stood next to him, looking at the old-timer like a parent silently scolding a child for something they didn't know they'd done. Boots appeared unaffected and sat motionless in his weathered chair.

"I can't believe you're not doing anything."

"I think you're mistaken . . . I'm doing something. Sitting here enjoying the view."

"You know what I mean, Boots. Jack could be hurt out there. Or worse, he could be . . ."

"He's fine. Like I say, a little time getting beat down may be all he needs."

"He's not that type of guy. He can't survive out there."

"I guess we'll find out, huh?"

She was incredulous. Frustrated at the old man's inaction. He sat there with the power to go after Jack, to bring him back, but did nothing. Boots read her mind.

"No fun, is it, waiting for someone to move?"

"What do you mean?" she asked.

"You know."

She did. She thought of herself, wasting so much time as her life seeped away. Relinquishing her own strength, her own happiness. Sitting idly by as her years rolled on. The accusation lacerated her and awakened her at the same time. She looked at Boots and nodded her head.

Boots's stern eyes softened as he looked back.

"Why you want him back so much? Huh? He seemed like he didn't know how to treat you."

"He's my husband. Why wouldn't I want him back?"

"Just figured you'd like it this way . . . maybe not?"

Laura thought about the stinging words. Stinging because they had passed through her mind before.

"What . . . what is it? Duty? You want him back because you think you have to?"

"No, that's not it."

"Aww . . . I get it. You're a romantic."

She stood motionless, hurt, defensive. "He's a good man."

"You say so."

"I know so."

"Then let me tell you something, Laura. If that be the case . . . then maybe he needs this. To get broken. To see that there is more than him to think about."

"He'll die out there, Boots!"

"You don't know that. Ain't going to happen if you would just listen."

Laura was a mess. Her frantic mind going haywire. She searched for normalcy, for understanding. This calmer-of-the-storms just sat there spitting chew without a care in the world while chaos was forming all around him. She wished she could will him to action, but he just kept the impish grin on his face.

"Tell you what," he started, his eyes reflecting a twinge of sympathy at her anguish, "when it cools down, I'll go get him. Bring him back, and we can start this all over again. I don't know what you expect to find when he's back, but I'll bring him back."

She paused.

"Thank you," she said with a whisper.

"What are you hoping to get back? That's the question you need to ask."

"What do you mean?"

"You holding out for him? Think he'll come back fixed? That he'll look at you and mend his ways?"

"I don't know."

"But that is what you want, ain't it? Deep down, that is what this is all about? You don't want the Jack back that was just here, you want the Jack back that walked out a long time ago."

She rubbed her hands together slowly. A nervous tick. She knew Boots was right. That was what this whole vacation-turned-survivor-camp had been about. She wished to find the one she lost years ago. In her heart, she always wished the person coming back to her every day, whether it was from work or a trip, was the man she remembered, who cared about her. Laura eyed Boots. For his rugged and brutish exterior, he could lay bare the soul and spread it out before a person like a potluck dinner.

Boots came up to her and put his dirty hand on her shoulder. She could feel his pulse in his hand, a slow, faint drumming reminiscent of a thumping grandfather clock.

"Let me ask you something, Laura," Boots said, his voice soft as a whisper. "Are you willing to do what it takes to get what you want? You willing to put yourself out there to help get back what's been lost?"

A tear fell down her cheek. She nodded her head while staring at the ground beneath her feet.

"Okay, then you need to trust me. I got it all worked out. Jack will be all right. When all is said and done, you'll get what you've been hoping on."

Boots removed his hand and returned to his chair.

Laura walked back inside and sat down at the table, resuming her gaze out the front window for any sign of a lonesome wanderer in the distance. Molly sat quietly sipping her water.

"What he say?" she asked.

"That he'll go after him."

"When, now?"

"Later, when it cools down. I think Boots wants Jack to suffer. I don't know why."

"He's got a bit of a sick streak in him, doesn't he?"

"I think so."

"I'm sure Jack will be okay."

"I hope so."

They sat in silence.

"It would be fun to be there when Boots finds him, huh?"

Laura managed a shallow smile. "Yeah, it would be."

The spider sat on his chest, rubbing its front legs together in gentle rhythm. Jack opened his eyes and froze, his heart in his throat. The spider stared back at him with eager eyes as it reveled in the fear it created. This tiny soldier of fortune.

"Where're you headed, Jack?" it asked with a voice he recognized but could not place. A distant remembrance.

"Home," Jack whispered.

"That's a long way. You know you'll never make it."

"I can make it."

"No, you won't. Why'd you leave Laura behind?"

"She didn't want to come, it was her choice."

"Was it really?"

"Yes."

The spider crawled slowly up his chest. Its fat body buoyed by eight points of creepiness. Jack could see the hair on its legs move in the air stirred by his own breath. He wanted to move but couldn't.

"Why don't you love her?"

"Who?"

"Laura."

"I do."

"No you don't. Admit it, you're glad she's not here."

Jack didn't answer. He didn't want to. He didn't want to hear himself say it.

"So you think this is your new life? Out here running on your own? What happens when you get home?"

"We go back to living."

"That's not what you want, is it, Jack?"

"Yes."

"You sure about that?"

"Yes."

"I don't believe you. There's a piece of you that wants this to go on, isn't there?"

"No."

"Stop lying to me, Jack!"

The spider crawled a few inches more. Its front leg reached out and started stroking Jack's bottom lip in slow, tantalizing motions. He could feel the coarseness of its hair, the sound of it stroking the stubble on his chin. Jack tried to breathe but couldn't.

Panic.

"What do you want, Jack?"

"I don't know."

"A new life? The old one? You want it to end right now?"

"I don't know."

"Really?"

"I . . . I . . ."

"You what?" it whispered.

"I . . . don't . . ."

The spider moved slowly. Its front legs worked at Jack's lips and pried his mouth open like a dentist performing a root canal. Jack could feel the sensation of pipe cleaners brushing against his teeth and on his tongue. The spider crawled into his mouth, the body crammed into the opening. A scream echoed in Jack's throat but had no escape.

He awoke and vomited on the rock floor. Jumping up, he ran his hands frantically over his clothes and danced around the cave, looking for the bug. He was alone. Wiping the vomit from his mouth, he tried his best to slow his racing heart. It was a dream. There was nothing here but him and silence.

I'm going crazy, he thought.

He didn't sleep the rest of the day. Watching the sun set over the western hills, he felt the phantom scratches of imaginary insects crawling inside his clothes.

He waited for nightfall to leave the cave. Several times during the day he had stepped out to survey the ridge and plot his way down, formulating his plan and gearing himself up for another trek in the dark.

The stars were out and the moon illuminated his path through the desert. He didn't run tonight. His muscles were sore, and fatigue racked his body. The sound of crunching dust below his shoes beat a cadence with his heart, and he marched on.

Several hours later, his heart skipped as he saw a sign of civilization.

A road.

Two lanes of paved blacktop running perpendicular to his path. He quickened his pace and jogged up to the pavement, standing on the shoulder.

Jack thought for a moment that he would see his rental car still sitting on the side of the road, but he knew this was foolish. He had no idea if this was the same stretch of highway, and so after looking down both horizons, he tried to knock the irrational thoughts of finding the broken-down Mustang out of his mind. He sat down on the shoulder and rested, trying to suppress the feeling that he was almost home. Almost done.

He recalled the night this all began, sitting on the center line and wishing for a quick end to it all. He was happy that he was alone. No burden of another's suffering on his conscience. For all he knew, Laura was resting peacefully in the bed in the back of Boots's cabin. Sure, she'd probably fumed at being left, but the way she got on with the old man, she more than likely spent the day on his front porch listening to stories, like a cheap lemonade commercial.

Jack felt the dimples in the road as they rested under the white shoulder stripe. Unchanging.

He thought about which way to go. The road must have led out from some town, or was on its way to one. Picking the wrong direction could kill him, leading him farther into the desert and away from people. Or he could keep going on the path he'd chosen, cutting cross-country toward the east. The only certainty he had was that he was not going to go back.

He got up and crossed the road, delaying his choice for those fifteen steps. The blackness of the night gave no indication of city lights on any horizon. It was a shot in the dark. A simple decision with the greatest ramifications. He stood there for several minutes, the supposed self-made man unable to choose his fortune. And then he saw it. Slowly building like a halo over the southern horizon. A white haze that grew in intensity until two halogens popped up over the road. A car. Driving fast and headed his way.

Excitement filled his heart as he pondered this development. He started thinking of rescue, but as the car approached, mile after mile, his stomach rose into his chest. The hair rose on the back of his neck with each passing second until it told him to move his feet. Whatever was coming down the road was forcing foreboding before it. Fear ran through his body and Jack knew that he needed to get off the road, to run as fast as he could east into the desert. His muscles ached and the sweat poured down his face as he ran, but it was as if his feet were in quicksand. Jack spotted a large boulder several yards ahead. With his body screaming at him, he leaped behind the boulder as the black pickup truck roared past. Jack cautiously peeked back at the road.

The truck went by the place he had been standing minutes before. The black pickup. He recalled Molly's story, the sadistic kidnapper. The black pickup. What was this twisted narrative he was being forced to partake in?

As soon as Jack's muscles began to ease their tension, he saw the brake lights turn on. The truck stopped in its tracks a quarter mile down the road. Then the white lights of its reverse gear kicked on as it squealed backward down the asphalt. Fear smothered Jack as he brought his legs in and cowered behind the rock.

The truck stopped. Suddenly a bright halogen light illuminated the desert in a narrow swath. The driver had gotten out and was using a flood lamp to look for something. His back to the boulder, Jack could see a beam of light pass over him to the left and disappear into darkness, the shadow of the rock shielding his presence from the giant flashlight. The beam disappeared for several minutes and Jack braved another peek.

The driver was on the other side of the road, several hundred yards off, searching with his light. Jack looked at the pickup idling on the highway a football field away. He could run for it, jump in the truck, and take off. Home free. But what if the guy had a gun? All it would take would be one noise, one pass of the lantern, and he would be spotted. He doubted he had the strength or speed to make it.

Suddenly his own position felt exposed. He looked east but could find no better cover. He wanted to run, farther into the desert. To find a better hiding spot. But again, the fear of being spotted filled every ounce of his being. He huddled himself down behind the boulder.

The light returned to his side of the road, and Jack thought he could make out the clicking sound of feet on pavement below the idling engine sound. He was in full-blown panic, waiting for the beam to stop on his position, for the boogeyman to come and do his work. But it never came.

Jack heard the sound of a car door slam, then the engine engage. The truck drove up the highway until the taillights faded from view.

He waited awhile to move, remembering every bad horror movie he had ever seen, expecting the truck to be lurking out of view, ready to fire up and chase him once he got up. But out here, there was no place to hide a truck. Boots was right. *Out here, you can see 'em coming.*

Jack stood, brushed himself off, and walked into the night. His heart rate settling back down as he thought about the irony of it all: he was now reciting Boots's lines.

Laura stared up at the darkness of the ceiling. Her thoughts drifted to earlier times of life back home with Jack. She missed him. She couldn't force herself to write him off. To hate him. No, her heart was attached to him no matter how hard she tried to think otherwise.

She had missed him for a long time. Longer than just this day. She couldn't remember how long.

The silence of the desert was all consuming. She felt so small, tucked away in this unseen corner of the world without relief from the loneliness. All she wanted was simple. She didn't want all the things that Jack's career afforded them. She just wanted someone to sit across from her at the dinner table and talk with her. To listen to her. To be interested in what she was thinking.

She had put her life on hold for him. Supported him emotionally and invested all she had into him. But as he climbed, he seemed to grow tired of her. She was of little value to what he now put his worth into. She felt that down to her bones. And she cried.

Where was he? Sitting out in the dark? Alone on some rock, looking up at the stars and basking in his freedom? Was he now happy? Running free on his own terms. She thought of her last words to him. "Don't say 'we.'" They had always been an "us," or so she had always thought.

The idea of him dead or dying out in the vast Mojave was something she would not entertain in her mind. No. He was well. Laura couldn't imagine him any other way. She relied on Boots's promise that he would go get him. That everything would be all right.

She got up and walked quietly through the cabin, fetched some water, and walked back toward the bedroom. Molly was sound asleep on the couch. This little vagabond running wild in a madman's world. Laura stopped and adjusted the covers on the young girl before heading back to bed. Back to the endless racing of her mind. Back to her loneliness. She stopped herself and decided to sit at the end of the couch next to Molly's feet. She just did not feel like being alone. No, she had had enough of that feeling.

The cave welcomed him that night with open arms. It was now his home. His hideout. His refuge. Colten could no longer go back to Goodwell. His days manning the gas station were done. He thought of this as a good turn of events.

Killing the cop had thrown everything into helter-skelter. It left him ill-planned for life as a fugitive. Had he thought it out better, he would have stocked supplies to hold out, but as it was, he was weakly equipped. The store would be watched. He couldn't go back. It would be instant capture.

Driving up to the next town wasn't a possibility either. On the roads he would be a sitting duck. He had been too careless that afternoon after the cop, driving like a madman late into the night looking for the girl, stopping and searching every slight movement that had caught his eye. He was playing with fate out there. Better to be up here in his cave. In his tomb.

It was dark. Cold. Empty.

Colten thought about sleeping in the truck, but after sitting in it all day, he had to get out and stretch his legs. He walked to the back of the cave and felt the chain in the wall. He rubbed the clasp in his hands, trying to catch the latent feel of its last occupant. He had been so close. He remembered kneeling in this very same spot. A missed opportunity. He hated himself at that moment as much as he hated anything.

He lay back on the stone floor and lit a cigarette. The white smoke escaped his lips and hung in the air above his head. The crack in the rock above him exposed a small sliver of the night sky, and he could see a couple stars shining down on him. Two celestial observers of his depravity. How much had they seen in the time since he opened the cave for business? Enough, he thought. And they burned on without ceasing, uncaring of the carnage he unleashed in this corner of the universe. No, nothing up there cared what he thought up.

"You're not getting sentimental on me, are you?" Seth said. He was seated by the entrance, watching Colten, supine on the floor.

"No."

"You have to keep on track. Focused. This is where many have been lost before."

"I know."

Colten thought of others in the past that were in his line of "work." They were all known because they had all been caught, usually by some stupid twist of fate or idiotic miscalculation. Much like the one he had performed on the highway today. He thought about the cop looking up at him from the hood of the cruiser, looking at him as she resigned her soul to her inevitable fate. He had taken no joy in it. She had not given him anything to bask in. She had kept her secrets, and died without pleading.

It would be his mistake. The Grand Mistake.

"You need to get your rest and then, in the morning, find that girl."

"I know."

"You can't give up on that."

"I know."

Colten took another drag of the cigarette. He couldn't get the scene with the cop out of his mind. He kept going back to his reaching up to the visor to pull the license. If he had not been panicked, if he had not been pushed into hysteria, he would have been fine.

"It's your fault, you know, why I'm messed up now."

"Why's that?" Seth asked as he got comfortable.

"If you hadn't been pushing me, getting me all worked up. I could have thought clearly. Been thinking straight."

"You want to blame me for this?"

"Yeah . . . why not."

Seth stood up and walked over to Colten. He stared down at the killer with an unearthly malice. Colten could feel the seething hatred pour from the man like a breeze chilled to absolute zero.

"You need to remember something. You are nothing without me. You are just a puppet. A piece of meat. You are in this 'mess' because of your stupidity. You have everything you have had because of me."

Colten put his cigarette out beside him but kept looking up. "All right," he said with a subtle attempt at sarcasm.

The man bent down low, his mouth next to Colten's ear. "I can kill you anytime I want. I could do it now. Reach down your throat. Grab your spine and rip it out. It means nothing to me. Just remember that."

An involuntary shiver ran through Colten. "All right, I got it."

"Good."

The man stood and walked to the cave entrance. "Now you get some rest. Tomorrow, this gets resolved."

Pegasus looked down on the lonely wanderer trekking the blackness of the desert night. Jack trudged on, always hopeful that the next rise would reveal salvation, but it never came. He began to question himself, his decision. He thought of the bed in the back of Boots's cabin, of Laura sleeping soundly, and longed to take off his shoes and crawl in bed with her. To experience the feeling of a long sleep. But the sagebrush proved a poor bed, and so he kept walking.

As he crested the ridge, he saw in the starlight a dry creek bed running off into the distance a hundred feet below him. He gazed with wanting eyes at the former home of a running river. His mouth yearned for just a taste of liquid, anything to beat the heat he was feeling.

He started the descent into the valley, recalling the hunting expedition with Boots. Yes, he would have even welcomed the old man into his company right now. The loneliness of this adventure, and the uncertainty of how it would turn out, made Jack long for a guide. Someone to lead him home. Anyone.

His thoughts jolted when his foot slid out from beneath him. The rocks below broke away and he clawed at the ridge wall. Kicking and scratching, Jack fought against the mini rock slide, trying to get a foothold but found none. He slid, and tumbled down.

Rolling, he could feel rocks hitting every part of his body. His back, his face, his back again. Jack slammed into the valley floor and laid spread out, his face in the dirt. It felt as if he had been beaten with a pillowcase filled with bars of soap. He tried to lift his head but couldn't, the fatigue and the beating had taken all his energy. He simply closed his eyes and passed out.

51

Molly got up in the middle of the night to grab some water. She filled a glass from the hand pump, took a sip, and turned around. Boots sat across the dark room staring at her. He seemed to look right through her. She felt exposed, examined. Like she had when the old man had found her in the cave. His stare made her feel uneasy.

"Dark night," he said.

"Yeah."

"Why don't you sit a bit, keep me company."

She thought he could sense her apprehension, but he motioned to her to sit on the couch across from him, and she crossed the room with short, deliberate steps. She settled down, doing her best to occupy as little space as possible. Boots just stared at her from his chair, his eyes penetrating her skin. She felt as if she was being weighed and measured, her heart judged right before her.

"You know, I thought you'd be the one to go running off in the night."

"Me?"

"Yeah, you."

"Well . . ." She paused. "I think we both know where that got me."

Boots smiled. "Yeah. But still, you got that fire burning in you.

That wanderlust. Every day you stay here, safe, I can't but think you'll forget the mess you were in a little bit more and more, begin thinking that now you're smarter. Won't get duped again. Head right back out there toward the west."

Molly swallowed hard. He was right. When she was rescued from the cave, she wanted nothing more than to run back to her mother's arms. Now slightly removed from immediate danger, her thoughts started drifting again to the excitement of LA and all the dreams she thought it held. She was as those on a ship who pray to the heavens when a hurricane hits, but then pull out the jet skis when the waters calm.

"Maybe I'll just stay here."

"Naw, this ain't no squatter's camp. Just a place to stop, sort things out, then move on."

"Works for you though."

Boots sighed. "Yeah, works for me."

She took another sip from the glass. "So you think I should go back home?"

"Doesn't really matter what I think, now, does it?"

Molly thought about the question.

"I can't make you go back. I can take you only so far. Columbus is much too far to walk." He chuckled. "You have to decide to go back."

"Is this the point where you tell me that when I'm older, I'll understand?"

"Naw, I ain't going to lay that on you."

"Good. I get tired of that."

"I can imagine."

She relaxed some more on the couch. Her nervousness releasing as she realized that Boots wasn't going to pull the "Grandpa" talk on her. She drank some more water and cleared her throat. "I'm afraid to go back."

"Why's that?"

"I don't know . . ."

"Bad stuff happen there?"

"No, it's just . . ."

"What?"

"Admitting to myself that I was wrong. That I'm not strong, that I'm not who I thought I was."

"There are worse things to realize in this life."

"I don't know if I can cope with it. It's embarrassing, the thought of going back."

"Ain't nothing to feel bad about, Molly. Worse will be waking up one day, years from now, wishing you had gone back. Bad thing about mistakes: you keep making more by not fixing the first ones."

"I didn't think it was a mistake . . . until I hit Vegas."

"I'm sure you thought it was wrong the whole way, deep down. You just kept pushing it down till it all got out of control."

She exhaled slowly, exorcising the thought from deep within her. "Yeah, I suppose you're right."

They stared at each other across the dark spaces.

"I have never been as scared as I was in that cave, Boots."

"I can imagine."

She stared at her hands, which had begun healing back to their teenage smoothness. They shook every time she thought of Colten. Boots walked over and sat next to her, taking her hands into his. His old, calloused palms encapsulating hers.

"There is evil in this world, Molly. You've seen it now. You stared into its eyes. Ain't nothing to be ashamed of. It changes the way you see the world." Boots seemed to drift in thought as he said the words. "Going home ain't mean you're broken, ain't mean you're not who you thought you were. It just means the world ain't like you thought it was."

Molly looked at the old man with tears in her eyes.

"But you're just as strong as when you left home. Stronger now. Wiser. Place to use that ain't found out west. Naw, way to be strong is to go back home. That will prove how strong you are."

He gave her hands a gentle squeeze, and then wiped the tear that rolled down her cheek. He stood and walked slowly out the front door into the night.

Molly remained on the couch as Boots's words floated through her soul.

The next morning Boots led the mare out of the stable and brought her around to the front of the cabin. It was early, the sun just starting to shine over the east. Laura walked out onto the porch clumsily, as she had not been able to sleep all night.

Boots climbed up onto the saddle and looked down at the tired woman before him. "You should get in and get some rest. I'll be gone awhile. Time to go get Jack."

"Can I come with you?"

"Naw . . . the horse can't pull us all, and I'm thinking Jack won't be up for walking once I find him."

"Are you sure you can find him, Boots?" Laura clasped her arms around her waist. She had cried herself dry. "Are you sure he is going to be okay?"

Boots didn't say anything as he led the horse away from the cabin.

Laura watched him disappear into the east. She stood there waiting as if the old man would turn and give her an answer.

Jack could see the shimmering forms through his eyelids. The dancing shades of horror, twisting and turning over the hot sands and rock, like magic water over the dry creek bed. The heat was unbearable, and he thought of only water. A few hours earlier he had attempted to climb down the shallow ravine in hopes that the river bed might hold some moisture. Now he was here, exhausted and battered to the point of immobility, waiting for death. And death seemed to be unfolding in the distance like a cabaret dancer enthralled in a sensual dirge.

He could see them more clearly now, the shapes of shadows peeking back at him. They grew in number each minute, straining their necks at the human wreckage before them, jostling each other for a better view.

The whispering breeze.

The canyon walls began crawling with shades. The rock bands of tans and reds slowly morphing into darker hues of black as the crowd flowed into this sandstone theater. Jack could feel his heart quicken but could not move. He could feel the swirling commotion around him, gathering, intensifying, but was unable to respond. The shadows grew more agitated as they began to fight with each other.

Jack strained to push himself up but only managed to make

it to his elbows. The shadows paused in their swirling to watch him. He gave a small grunt as he reached out with his right hand, grabbed some earth, and pulled himself forward a few inches. It took every ounce of energy he had in him. The sun had done its work . . . he was completely exhausted.

Wincing in pain, he threw his left hand out and tried to pull himself a bit more but could not. His body slumped and his consciousness hung by a thread. In a whirlwind of a thousand voices, the shadows' laughs rushed down the canyon walls like water over a dam.

Then stillness. Nothingness.

"Hey, Jack."

A cool air drifted over his body while stale air filled his nose, suffocating.

"You're in a bit of a pinch, aren't you? Miles away from nowhere."

Jack lay without movement. He was too tired and too scared to move, as if playing dead would keep the bear from devouring him. He could feel a presence kneeling next to him. Then he was being shoved, rolled onto his side. His eyes fluttered open.

The man from the cabin. The midnight visitor.

"Don't feel like talking much, huh? That's okay by me. You don't seem like the kind of guy that had anything of substance to share anyway." The man stood and stretched his back. "What are you doing out here?"

"J-j-just . . . want to g-get home."

"Naw, you don't want that." Seth's face twisted into a sneer. "That's what y'all say. *I want to go home.* You're out here for a reason. You just haven't figured it out yet."

Jack forced his eyelids to stay open a sliver, just enough to see him. Seth was visibly becoming bored with the conversation as he walked a couple steps and sat down on a rock.

"I've been out here a long time, Jack. I've seen plenty of people just like you. What? You think you're unique. Huh? Yeah, I guess you all do. You ain't nothing, Jack. Nothing. You all come running from something, something bigger than you, and then you come out here and think you are bigger than you are. Yeah, that must be it. You think you're something bigger than you are.

"Probably think the world spins around you, don't you, Jack? Think you're at the center of everybody's mind. When you going to get it, Jack? You ain't nothing. Ain't even worth me coming out here messing with you. Almost a waste of my time."

Jack closed his eyes and gripped the ground.

Scared.

Anticipating something but not knowing what.

Intimidated. He knew the man could take a rock and smash his head, and he had not the strength or courage to even lift his hands to ward off the blow. He was five years old, hiding under the blanket from the boogeyman.

Fear is the acute sensation of hope leaving the body.

"There was a guy much like you awhile back. Came out here mountain climbing, though the fool knew nothing about no climbing. Arrogant. You know what that fool done? Fell and broke his back. Stuck up there in the rock and nobody knew he was there. Just sat there for days blinking up at the sky, spitting his own blood out of his mouth. How do you think he felt then, Jack? Probably pretty small, huh?

"Yeah, ain't had much fun when we found him though. Ain't much fun when they got no hope left, when they beg you to end it all right quick. Can't find no joy in that." The man drifted off into a sick remembrance, then jumped back with a laugh.

"Hey, Jack, what you think went through his mind when that rope snapped? I'll tell you what probably happened. Fool got stuck up in a tight spot. Dangled there for a while. Too scared to go up higher, more than likely . . . didn't know enough how to get back down. Probably got hungry, night coming on. Bats start flying around his head. Maybe hitting his legs. Wind pick up and get up under his skin. He lost hope real quick, more than likely. Thought he could cut that rope and end it real fast. Probably reached down into his boot, grabbed the knife that was on him, put it up over his head, and cut that line."

Seth's gaze drifted off as if he was seeing the memory play out before him on a distant screen. He soon snapped back to the present and looked down at Jack. "Problem is, fool wasn't high enough to kill himself. Only broke his back. Came near to folding in half. Yeah, can't have too much fun when that is all you're given."

The hot sand filled Jack's nostrils as he remained motionless on the ground. He thought if he kept his eyes shut, the man would leave, disappear, stop existing.

"So what say you, Jack? You just going to lie there and play dead or are you going to give us something to work with?"

"I haven't done anything to you," Jack whispered, but the sound was further muted by the rock his face was half buried in.

"What's that?"

"I haven't done anything to you."

"Haven't done anything to me? Come on, Jack, didn't I say this ain't about you? Get that through your mind . . . this ain't about you! You're nothing."

"I'm not going to fight you."

"You have to have a little bit of spine in you. Something inside that thinks you might get out of this. Something that you're clinging to."

Silence. The man spit and the dry earth hissed.

"Pathetic. You really got nothing, huh. What about that sweet thing you drove in here with. I bet she'd put up a good fight . . . unless of course she pegged her hopes on you. If she did, she'd probably beg me to end it right quick too."

Laura. Jack's thoughts returned to her, mixed with the horror story relayed to them by Molly. Was this the man who kidnapped her? Had kept her hidden away and came within minutes of strangling her? Jack's rage began to build as he thought about Laura in that situation. He could feel blood flowing through his limbs, his adrenaline began pumping.

"Ahhh . . . so she does mean something to you," the man said as he stood up and looked around. "So where is she, huh? Did she fall down this canyon wall too?"

He walked around, peeking behind the rock he was just sitting on.

"No . . . she's not here is she? You left her. You left her behind." Realization dawned on the man.

"She's back at Boots's place, ain't she? Wow, Jack, that's something. I can't say I've seen that happen before."

Jack could feel something move, subtle, as if an invisible hand began pushing the watching shades back up the ridge and sweeping them away. He looked up at the man, whose gaze was fixed on the western sky.

"Got to be moving on, Jack. You're not worth my time. But thanks for the news about your woman." He bent down and patted Jack on the head like he would a dog. "Yeah, I think that might be the best news I heard in awhile."

Jack could hear the man's footsteps wander off as he was left alone on the valley floor.

"Get up, you got work to do!" Seth shouted as he walked into the cave, appearing as if out of thin air.

Colten got to his feet and rubbed the sleep out of his eyes with his nicotine-stained fingers. It was dark except for a sliver of light from the roof crack. It was easy to lose a sense of time in here, one of the perks he found when he had first discovered it. Unfortunately he had not planned on having the effect work him over.

"What time is it?"

"Doesn't matter, I got a surprise for you."

"You found the girl?" Colten blurted, almost dropping the lighter as he prepared to get his morning fix.

"No, but I think I found something that will make a good replacement."

"What do you mean?"

"There's a place not too far from here. There's a woman there, abandoned. Left alone."

"Out here?"

"Yes."

"How'd you know this?"

The man walked out of the cave and Colten quickly followed. "How'd you know this!"

"Just take it and use it. You don't have much time."

"What do you mean?"

The man spun on his heels and stared at Colten. His black eyes breaking the will of the homicidal maniac. Colten's legs felt weak, like he did when he was ten and his old man would start whipping him.

"Do you need an explanation for everything?"

"No."

"All right. It's enough to know that the old man who owns the cabin is off on a pointless errand. The woman is there. All you need to do is drive down there and pick her up. You can do that now, can't you?"

"Yeah."

The man started walking away again toward the two-lane down the mountain.

"But what about the girl? Are we going to find the girl?"

"Consider her lost. You had your chance, you blew it."

Colten stood motionless, a worker given a list of instructions but not knowing how to turn the machine on. "So how do I find the place?"

"Just start driving," the man replied as he disappeared from view. "You'll find it soon enough."

"Where you think you're going, Jack?"

Jack struggled to open his eyes. A combination of thirst, exhaustion, and blinding sunlight made this almost impossible. It took him awhile to get his bearings. It must be midday, and he was lying on his stomach eating dust, staring at a pair of old cowboy boots.

"That was pretty stupid there, Jack, coming out here all by yourself," Boots said as he squatted on his haunches, pouring a small stream of water from his canteen over Jack's cracked face.

Jack worked to lift his head off the ground enough to capture some of the water in his cheek.

"You don't know the way out of here. Only thing you can do is get lost and die."

"I . . . I'm . . ." Jack's parched throat was unable to let his voice pass.

"What's that?" Boots said, pouring more water onto Jack's face and into his mouth.

"I'm going . . . for help . . ."

"Help? Help? What you think I've been giving you?"

"I . . . I want to . . . get home."

"Home? Huh . . . What kind a home you got, Jack? Especially one where you leave your wife behind? Don't sound like no home I'd want to go back to."

The accusation was quick and brutal. Jack had left Laura behind in the cabin. He told himself that her staying was her choice, that he would come back for her. But her staying allowed him what he wanted, to run off on his own, unencumbered by her. No matter how he tried to justify his actions in his head, he came to the same conclusion. He had left her. Not just in the cabin, but before that. He had left her long ago. The pain of this epiphany was soon eclipsed by the pain of a boot heel pressed into his lower back.

"You want me to put you out of your misery right here, Jack?" Boots said, pressing harder with his foot into Jack's right kidney. "Naw, that would be too easy. How about I just rough you up a bit? Maybe that will get you thinking straight."

He started to circle around Jack's near-lifeless body on the desert floor like a vulture. With a quick half step, Boots kicked Jack in the side of the stomach, causing him to temporarily leave the soil and crash back down.

"Yeah, dying would be too easy. That's the safe way out, ain't it. You don't have to worry about nothing no more then, huh?" Another quick kick in the side made Jack vomit what water he'd been able to swallow just a minute earlier.

"Look at you," Boots whispered, squatting down again next to Jack, "puking on the ground like an animal. What are you, Jack? You think you're Superman?" Boots tipped his brimmed cowboy hat back and gazed off toward the distant ring of mountains. "Naw, you're not Superman. I ain't never seen no superman. Seen plenty who thought they were, no doubt about that. But they all end up the same way. Rolling in their own puke, unable to wipe the spit from their lip." He poured some more water onto Jack's face as he went on. "Naw, the way I see it, ain't no superman . . . never will be. Just men butting their heads against a brick wall, wondering why their skulls ache. Kinda like you, Jack. Except you just can't stomach the fact that maybe that there wall was built by someone tougher than you."

Boots looked at the ground next to Jack. There were black scuff marks and footprints.

"Looks like you had some company here, Jack," he whispered. "You best be thankful I'm here now. Who knows what's out there that would like a piece of you."

Jack found the strength to push himself up, and he sat on the ground. His head was spinning and he felt like he might pass out again. Boots caught his shoulder and poured more water down his throat. He revived quickly, and though his head pounded like a jackhammer, the cobwebs in his mind started to clear. Boots sat down on a rock across from him, seemingly enjoying the train wreck of humanity before him.

"You're a mess, Jack. Why'd you do this?"

The words echoed in Jack's skull. *Why'd you do this?* The same words Laura asked in the car. The same question he asked himself every day of his life.

"You ever read the Scriptures, Jack? Huh? No, probably not. Ain't no one reads them no more. But you remind me of this man, much like you. He was pigheaded too. Ain't listen to reason. It took an angel coming down to whoop him good to get his head on straight. Maybe that's all you need. Someone come and beat you down a bit." Boots took a swig of water from the canteen. "What you say, Jack? You want me to beat the stupid out of you right here?"

Jack remained silent.

"You think I'm too old?" Boots smiled, his grizzled features bearing malice and lightheartedness mixed together. "Maybe so. I've been in plenty of scraps though. Brought down bigger mules than you, that's for sure."

Jack looked at Boots. He wanted nothing more than to jump up and drive his fist square into the old man's face. He scripted out the scenario in his mind, unrelenting, swinging until Boots's blood mixed with the rocks and he laid there begging for mercy. He would keep punching, pouring out all his pent-up frustration onto this bag of bones.

"Ahhh . . . thinking up something, eh, Jack? Just wishing you had the strength to smash me in with that there rock? What's that gonna do? You'll still be stuck out here, no place to go. You're trapped, ain't you?" Boots smiled again. He tossed the canteen over to Jack and it landed in his lap, followed by a chunk of dried meat. "You better get your strength up. We need to start heading back before dark. It's a good thing you didn't make it too far. I didn't bring enough food for no camping trip."

From the top of the ridge, Jack could see the horse looking down on them. Boots stood up, grabbed Jack by the arm, and hoisted him up. They climbed out of the little valley, mounted the horse, and began the ride back.

Molly and Laura spent the day on the front porch. It had now become routine. The days had started to blend together, each passing hour melting into the one before. They tried hard to guess what day of the week it was, even made a little game of it, but ultimately decided that since there was no way to verify the answer, the game had little point.

Laura kept looking for the horse and riders to return, envisioning herself in some cheap dime-store romance waiting for her cowboy to come home. She couldn't explain why she felt a sense of calm come over her when Boots had left, but something about the old man's countenance had convinced her that he would return with Jack in good health.

Molly sat next to her, her dark hair blowing across her face. She had become a chatterbox now that they were alone, as if the men in the house had left her feeling unsure of her own voice. The girl started talking of home, and though she had been through a lot, a trauma that not too many people could fathom, she seemed to be returning to the same mall girl she might have been in Columbus.

Laura tried her best to listen, to keep the conversation going, mostly because she knew it offered a release for Molly, but her thoughts were in other places. Plus, out here in the desert, and with her own experiences the past week, she didn't feel like talking about the follies of teenage boys. No, her mind was on the quiet praying for Jack to come back in one piece.

The morning slowly gave way to day, when out in the distance the women could see something stirring. Faintly at first, the dust trail of a moving object appeared like pencil lead across a blank page.

"What is that?" Molly asked.

"I don't know."

Laura stood, put her hand to her head to shield the sun, and squinted her eyes. She fought to focus on the distant object until it became clear what it was.

"It's a car," she whispered, and then her excitement poured out. "It's a car!"

Molly stood up and imitated Laura. They felt like hugging each other. The ordeal was finally over. The rooster tail of dust grew larger as the vehicle sped across the desert. Closer and closer into view.

Ominous.

Malignant.

"That's not a car," Molly said, her exuberance subsiding. "It's a truck . . ."

"Are you sure?" Laura said, still trying to make out the details.

"Oh my . . . it's him . . . it's him!"

Molly grabbed Laura's arm and did her best to drag her into the cabin. The realization slowly dawned on Laura when she saw the horror on the young girl's face.

The pickup.

The man who had kidnapped Molly.

He had found them.

They got inside and slammed the door. Molly stood in the middle of the room screaming, looking frantically for a place to hide, a weapon, anything to protect her from what was coming. Laura grabbed her and tried to calm her down while working to quell the fear that was crawling on her own skin.

"What are we going . . . what are we going to . . ." Molly stammered frantically, unable to catch her breath.

"Shhh . . . calm down, you have to calm down."

"What are we going to do?"

"We gotta get out of here . . . we got to hide . . ."

Laura pushed Molly to the bedroom and toward the window facing the back, all the while looking around for inspiration, something that would jump up and tell her that everything would be all right. Some object of comfort. Molly stood ashen, staring back at Laura with eyes begging for rescue.

The women could hear the truck pull up outside.

"Shhh . . ." Laura whispered, as she placed one hand over Molly's mouth.

The girl nodded wide-eyed.

Fear.

Laura could feel it envelope the cabin. But there was no one else to face it for her. All these years of passively waiting in the shadows, leaning on other people's actions would not serve her now. Her father was not here, Jack was not here, and now Boots was gone. Staring at Molly's face, she could read the panic racing through the girl's mind and how this young soul was looking to her for resolution. For rescue. For determination. A position that Laura had shied away from most of her life.

But now it had arrived. Fear of harm mixed with the fear of standing strong.

They listened as the door of the truck opened and a man got out, his footsteps strutting up to the cabin door.

Laura removed her hand slowly from Molly's mouth and motioned for her not to move. The girl nodded again. Turning, Laura quietly walked out to the main room, careful not to make the old floorboards creak. She stared at the cabin door and imagined the evil on the other side just waiting to come in.

Colten stepped slowly onto the porch and tried to look into some of the windows, but the glare from the sun prevented him from seeing anything. He moved slowly.

He knew this was the place.

He had been led here.

The woman was inside.

Alone.

Acting calm, but with anticipation mounting in his blood, he knocked three times on the door.

The sounds reverberated through the cabin like the slow tap of a ball-peen hammer on hollow steel. Laura could feel the waves pass through her, settling in the base of her spine. Her stomach was forcing itself up into her throat. Her eyes darted around the room, from the couch, to the table, to the kitchen area, back to the door, looking for some source of salvation . . . a movie cliché of arrival and rescue. There was none.

It was just her and a homicidal maniac separated by a rotting cabin door.

Jack sat on the back of the horse, holding on to Boots, as the mare sauntered into the west, back to the prison that he could not escape from.

The breeze blew gently, and the smell of Boots filled his senses. It was surprising, half expecting the old man to smell of dirt and filth, he smelt like the pages of an old book from some second-hand shop.

The slow rhythm of the horse's cadence set him at ease, and Jack's mind slowly unwound. He could feel his strength returning to him, almost by mystery. He could not tell whether the little food that Boots had given him had restored his energy, or if it was the ride that infused him with newfound life. All he knew was that with each passing hoofbeat he felt better. Stronger. Restored.

The nagging question in the back of his mind surfaced as they walked on. "How's Laura?"

Jack wasn't sure if he wanted the answer. He wasn't ready to see his wife's eyes when they returned to the cabin. The silence. The glaring. The hopeless chance of trying to explain why he had done what he did. She would let him talk, but she wouldn't listen. He had abandoned her. He could see that now. In his determination to get out of the cabin, he had thought only of himself.

"She's fine," Boots replied. "Worried, but fine."

"I bet she's pretty mad."

"You think? Well . . . at least this walk taught you something. You're finally starting to get how other people feel."

Jack sat silently. It had been a long time since he empathized with Laura, had understood that she was her own thinking person, one with the same capacity to dream and wonder as he did. He just thought of her as a hanger-on to his ambition. One who should bask in his light as her benefactor.

"She say anything to you?" Jack asked, looking for some sign that the woman back at the cabin might be in a welcoming mood. Hoping.

"She asked me to come get you. Pleaded. Said you'd die in a heartbeat out here by yourself. That woman knows you pretty well, Jack."

The mare's head rocked with each step, an organic metronome through the desert.

"I can't believe you just left her, Jack. I'll tell you what kind of man does that . . . a fool. You remember when I first brought you here? 'Course you don't. You was half gone. I brought you in the cabin and started giving you some water. I filled up a quart jar from the hand pump and walked over to Laura, started pouring a bit in her mouth. You know what she does then? She opens her eyes after a small sip and says to me, 'No, give some to Jack, please.'

"You hear that? Woman there dying of thirst and she tells me to give you a drink first."

Boots spit to the side, his weight jerking the saddle, causing Jack to grab the old man for balance.

"Then what happens? I move over and start pouring some water down your throat. And you just keep drinkin'. No thought or mind for no other. Says more about you than you know."

Jack didn't respond. Though he didn't recall the incident, it didn't fall out of the realm of the possible. It certainly fit his nature, and he felt ashamed.

58

"Hello?"

Colten knocked again. No answer.

He stepped to the side of the door and looked in the window, cupping his hands to fight against the glare. He could see the kitchen with its small table, the couch. His eyes scanned the room, down the hallway. It was a small place, this should be easy.

He grabbed the door handle and tested it. Locked. Colten studied the doorjamb and saw that it was pretty weak. The age and rot of the place gave the cabin little strength.

He stepped back, raised his foot, and kicked at the door. The handle broke but the chain-lock held firm. The door parted a few inches. From inside he could hear a quick scream.

The prize.

He reached inside and felt for the chain but couldn't get it.

Laura saw Colten's fingers wiggle through the doorjamb. They resembled the legs of a spider feeling its way through the air. Catching her breath, she pounced forward, slamming her weight against the door, smashing his fingers in the process.

Screams of agony echoed through the desert emptiness.

Colten pushed against the door, doing everything possible to free his fingers pressed numb against the doorjamb. Laura stood on the other side, all her energy used in keeping it closed. He could hear her breaths, her exertions.

"I'm going to kill you! You know that, right!" he screamed through clenched teeth, his eyes rolling to the back of his head as he tried to process the pain coursing through his hand. He put his shoulder into the door again and again, pulling on his trapped fingers. Finally they came free and the door shut securely in the jamb.

Colten fell back on the porch, clutching his hand, whimpering. Underneath the door he could see the faint shadow of Laura's feet. She was right there, inches away from him. His source of agony.

He stood and kicked the door with the rage of demons.

It flew open, knocking Laura back onto the kitchen table. It smashed apart as it broke her fall. She quickly regained her feet and stood facing him, a splintered leg from the table held firmly in her hand. She could feel a thin trickle of blood running from her hairline.

So this is how it starts, she thought.

A maniacal smile crossed his face.

"You? I know you," he said with a mix of surprise and sick fascination.

He took two steps forward, seemingly unconcerned with the weapon she had. She swung it quick, as if she had been anticipating the move for years, and landed the blow low on the side of Colten's knee. He buckled in pain and dropped to his knees. Laura brought the table leg back again, but before she could strike, Cole drove his fist into her stomach. She doubled over, and then he backhanded her across the head. The table leg went flying as Laura fell to the floor.

With his good hand, Colten grabbed Laura's ankle. She kicked at his arm with her free leg, but he would not let go. Colten's body was in such a state of shock that added pain had a diminishing effect. He refused to let go. Crawling on the ground like a wounded lizard, he fought the blows of the woman and pinned her to the ground. His fury out of control. He looked down into Laura's face.

"This is going to be good!" he whispered to her.

His hands began to strangle her by their own will as if possessed by something outside his body. He was in the zone. The perfect zone. This woman was done.

Then the noise.

"Hey!"

Colten looked up. Toward the back of the cabin.

There was *the girl*.

His lost adventure.

Running toward him.

The table leg held back in her hands like Big Papi swinging for the fences.

Colten's head tilted and his eyes widened in fascination as Molly swung the piece of wood across his face, his nose breaking on impact and spewing blood through the cabin. The shock of the blow sent him back through the doorway and rolling down the porch into the dust.

Molly helped Laura to her feet, the older woman's eyes showing the realization of death in them. The two women stepped to the door and looked outside.

Colten was staggering to his feet, his wounded hand trying to offer comfort to his busted nose as his frame tottered on his swollen knee. His whole body was in pain. He looked at them through swelling eyes. His body began to shake. His rage uncontrollable.

Laura took the table leg from Molly and started stepping through the door onto the porch. Molly stayed behind her.

"You need to get out of here!" she yelled, doing her best to sound strong.

"I ain't leaving."

"Get out of here!"

"This is just getting started!" Colten spit venom and blood onto the ground as he advanced to the porch. Laura swung the weapon but missed, the blow going wide and carrying her momentum with it. Colten grabbed her and threw her off the porch. Laura went crashing to the ground. Molly suddenly stood exposed, staring into the eyes of her kidnapper again.

"Remember me?" Colten said as he grabbed her hair with both hands, driving his knee into her abdomen. The girl crumpled before she knew what happened. Colten then cuffed her across the head, knocking her unconscious on the porch.

He turned to face Laura, who was just getting up off the ground. The wood was still in her hand.

Colten laughed. "Looks like we have a stand-off here."

Laura surveyed the scene. Molly lay on the porch, Colten's boot now placed gingerly over the girl's neck as one would squash a bug. She stood several steps away, bruised, scared, and shaking. Her eyes looked on the horizon. *Boots, Jack . . . where are you?*

"Ain't no one coming . . . it's just you and me now."

Laura tried to force words into her throat. Her adrenaline had already exhausted itself with the first round inside the cabin. She held the table leg more in self-defense.

"Get away from her," she stammered.

Colten put his hands up and smiled, lifted his boot, and stepped off the porch. "You say so."

Laura found herself moving backward with each advancing step of Colten.

"You ready for this?" he asked, savoring the moment that was unfurling before him. He could sense her apprehension. Her fear. Her intimidation.

Laura suddenly felt the truck grill pressed up against her back. There was no more space to retreat. She planted her feet and squeezed the piece of lumber in her hand.

"Yeah," she whispered, "I'm ready for this."

He tilted his head, blood dripping from his nose and mouth. The same sadistic grin on his face.

Laura prayed for Boots and Jack to emerge from the wasteland as she swung with all her strength.

Red hadn't eaten all morning. He was surprised he was hungry at all. But he was a big man, and big men, even in the hardest of circumstances, cannot forgo food for very long.

The night before he had thrown up his dinner by the subtle red glow of road flares when he arrived at the scene of his deputy's death. He had seen death before. Had seen carnage. But it was always detached. At arm's length. Here was his own . . . Officer PJ Morey. What was left of her.

He had got the call at 7:24 p.m., right before the last "Final Jeopardy" question on the TV. Red had sent James out looking for PJ when she hadn't radioed in for a while. James called him in shock . . . crying . . . screaming like a little girl.

"What's wrong, James?"

"Red . . . you got to get up here . . . she . . . PJ . . ."

Sounds of retching.

". . . she's . . . Red, she's just . . . !"

Red had left his cat Sox to lie in the faint shadow of the TV set and headed out to see what happened. He found James wandering along the shoulder overcome with shock and grief. He stopped his cruiser and got out.

"James . . . James!" Red yelled, pulling the deputy out of his delirium. "Where is she?"

James held up his trembling hand, his voice shaking. "O . . . ov . . . over there . . ."

Red walked over and saw what remained of Officer PJ Morey. Her body lying below the hanging front bumper of the smashed police car. A stream of blood darkened the pavement, stretching out. This beautiful young woman cut down, her life cut off.

That was where he had lost it. The mix of horror and beauty caused him to vomit as well.

He wiped the corners of his mouth and called to James. "Get some help up here, James. Doctor . . . ambulance . . . I don't know . . . just get someone."

"All right."

And that was the last memory he had of his young deputy. He and James waited for the ambulance from the safety of his idling police cruiser.

Now, Red walked down the aisle of the decrepit convenience store outside of Goodwell. He picked up a candy bar and marched to the back room, its door next to the cooler. James stood by the entry door, his gun out even though Red told him to keep it holstered.

"Cole! You back there? Cole!"

The chief punched the door open but the room was empty. He returned to the front of the store. Everything was still.

"You really think it was Cole done that?"

"I don't know, James, but he better be praying right now if he did."

He bit into the candy bar and chewed slowly. Reaching over the counter, he rifled through the stack of magazines next to the over-flowing ashtray. Just some celebrity gossip rags, with an outdoor one thrown in for balance.

"You ever see Cole go anyplace else?"

James scratched his head. "Not sure. I saw his truck one time up by Shim's place. But that must've been about a year ago."

Another bite of the candy. "I want you to go around here and talk to some folks. Find out if he's got a place he goes to, someplace he might be at right now."

"All right, Red."

James walked to his car and headed into town, leaving Red still standing at the counter. What was going on? Nothing ever happened like this out here. This wasn't supposed to happen. Cops around these parts grew old and bored; they weren't supposed to die young and brutal.

He couldn't get the vision of his deputy out of his mind. The once vibrant lady now gone to her eternal rest.

People feel more horror in the act of death than in death itself. The results are the same, dead. But the process is what got under people's skin. The method. And Red, through all his years in this line of work, had never seen a method such as what he saw on the highway.

He kept himself from breaking down. He wasn't that sort of guy, but sadness filled his heart and mixed with the anger welling up toward Cole. It had to have been him who did this. His was the last name spoken between the two cops. It was her last reported stop. It was him.

Red punched the rack display on the counter and a medley of lighters and air fresheners flew to the ground and splintered across the floor. If he found Cole, he was sure he would kill him on the spot.

He stepped over the mess he made and headed outside. The midday heat already setting the earth on fire. He got in the cruiser, but had no idea where he should head off to.

It took half a day to make it back to the cabin. It had not been as far as Jack had hoped. Part of him wanted it to be farther, a testament to his manhood that, despite the failed attempt, he had trekked a hundred miles through the wasteland, a story fitting for the annals of jailbreak folklore. It turned out to be about twenty.

Jack was also not in a hurry to confront Laura. Would she be grateful he was back? Or would she torment him with a cold silence that would leave him on edge, refusing to talk to him until right before he would go to sleep, knowing just the right time to torture a tired man. He didn't know what he was riding into.

He saw the cabin come into view and his heart sank. Back to whatever this was. They trotted into the dust behind the cabin and dismounted the horse.

Boots led the horse into the small pen, releasing the mare to its trough, and walked out.

Silence surrounded both of them.

Jack walked to the front of the cabin and noticed the busted door. Stepping inside, he called out Laura's name, and saw the shattered table. His gut clenched. He called out again. No answer.

He met Boots in the backyard, the old man standing next to a fence post, gazing west.

"Where's Laura?"

"Looks like she's gone, don't it?"

Jack looked over the small cemetery at the back of the house. There was a fresh layer of dirt in the back corner, crusted by the sun. He also saw a shovel sitting by the gate.

"Where is my wife?" Jack screamed.

"Maybe she ran off, you know, like you did." The old man seemed generally unconcerned.

"She wouldn't do that."

"Look, Jack, you left her here, remember? You're the one that ran off in the middle of the night like some fool. What? You think she should've sat around here waiting for you?" Boots spat on the ground and chewed on his lip as he looked Jack square in the eye. "You did, didn't you? Ha! You're a piece of work, Jack."

"Where is she, Boots?"

"Don't really know."

Jack looked back across the small cemetery plot and zeroed in on the back corner. The tilled soil beckoned his gaze, calling at his curiosity, his anger. "I don't believe you," he whispered.

"She didn't need to be here, Jack, never did. She could of gone back day one. She knew it, deep down she did. Nope, that ain't who she is, is it? Naw, she stayed on because of you, Jack. She thought she was supporting you, being what you needed, suffering for you. Then what did you do? You snuck off in the middle of the night like a coward. You left her here. With me? What kind of man does that, Jack?"

Jack kept staring, gazing at the dirt. Boots's words twisting his soul, springing forth rage from the deepest parts of his heart. Rage at this hermit who was playing God. Rage at his own selfishness. Rage at Laura for playing the role of the suffering saint.

Twisting, turning, the guilt tore into Jack's guts with each word from Boots. His life passed before his eyes in one fell swoop. His marriage, his home life, himself, all instantly destroyed by one stupid car ride to nowhere. He wanted freedom from what? Domestication? Support? Whatever at the moment seemed to stand in the way of his boundless ambition?

"She's a fine soul, Jack. Deserves much better in this life than to be a third wheel in your love affair with yourself. Yes sir, she deserves better than she got!"

Tearing at his insides like fingers through wet paper. He hated her for leaving him here, for going on without him. But didn't he do that to her? Now she was gone. What kind of twist of cosmic fate was this?

"You're glad she's gone? You wanted her gone deep down, didn't you?"

The corner field called out to him. He could see it in his mind. The story made sense. While he was gone, the crazy man had killed them both. Laura and Molly. He knew what had happened. They were buried in the back, in the plot, together. This truth made sense, it seemed rational to him.

This man wasn't in the business of saving people; he was in the business of pulling people into his sick whirlpool and putting them six feet under in his own morbid picture gallery.

It made sense to Jack, and that's all that mattered.

"What did you do to her, Boots?" Jack screamed again.

Boots looked down at his feet and spit between them. He had barely started to respond when the shovel crashed into the side of his face, smashing his jaw into countless pieces and knocking the old man off his feet. He looked up to see Jack standing over him, the shovel wielded like a baseball bat and that same nothingness in the eyes that he had witnessed before. The same nothingness that had driven Boots to the desert in the first place.

"You don't know what you doing, Jack!" Boots gasped.

Jack swung again, landing a blow to the old man's side.

The deed was done before Jack could realize what he did. The old Rasputin lay calm on the ground before him. One minute he was there spitting chew and venom and now he was gone. Just a pile of skin and beard. His life was over. Just like that.

The full weight of what he had just done flooded Jack's mind. He had murdered someone. Him . . . Jack . . . the businessman from Chicago. He shouldn't be here; he should be catching a flight to the East Coast to close some deal. How did he get caught up driving through the desert, stranded, kidnapped, widowed, and then murdering someone? Just last week he was a different person.

The rage left him, and he saw with clear eyes again.

He looked at the old man on the ground. It wasn't like the movies. It only took two swings, not a hundred.

"Boots . . . ," he said, throwing down the shovel. "Boots!"

He got down on his knees and tried shaking the hermit, but to no avail.

Boots was gone,

Jack was all alone.

A single speck in a sea of nothingness.

Suddenly, Jack could feel the wind shift at his back, and he could see his own shadow on the ground fade as the sunlight dimmed by degrees. The desert silence behind him was broken by the sound of a single pair of hands . . . clapping.

"Bravo, Jack . . . bravo," Seth whispered.

Jack spun on his heels and saw the man in the black shirt and pearl buttons, the same man from the canyon, leaning on one of the fence posts. Still wielding the shovel and half crazed, he pointed it at the man. Boots's blood dripped from the blade.

"You . . . you stay away from me!" Jack yelled.

"I ain't going to harm you, Jack. You did me a favor. That old man done outlived his welcome out here. You're a hero, Jack."

"He killed my wife . . ."

"Are you sure about that?"

"He . . . over there . . . buried her . . ." Jack's mind glazed over and he fought to fit two ideas together.

"Where? Over there, Jack? Ain't no one been buried in that place for a long time."

Jack looked back across the old cemetery plot. The far corner looked as even and smooth as the rest of the ground. But he saw it . . . he saw it before. He knew deep down what had happened.

"Looks like you might have messed up again, Jack. Trying to be John Wayne for a day, huh? Well, one thing's for sure. You killed old Boots dead. Ain't no doubt about that." The man started to walk slowly toward Jack, who raised his weapon again.

"I told you to stay away from me!"

"You shoulda realized, Jack . . . only a few things kept your life in order. Now they are gone. Vanished. You're on your own now."

"Get back!"

"You always thought you were a self-made man—"

"Stop . . . Get back!"

"Well, here you are, standing on your own."

The sky behind the man began to swirl in hues of black and gray. The shadows began to materialize and begin their slow dance of doom. All of them looked at Jack like a tasty morsel, a shell-shocked deer in the headlights of the devil's monster truck.

The shovel dropped from Jack's hand as the first shade grabbed his face. He could feel them pelting his body like hail. Gnashing at his nerves, driving him slowly into madness. They swirled around his body, creating a vortex that lifted him off his feet and slammed him into the side of the cabin, knocking the wind out of him.

Swarms of shadows raced over his body, absolute zero shocking his sweat-soaked skin. He could feel his muscles constrict and then relax again uncontrollably. He felt like he was being gutted from the inside out . . . his head ready to explode.

Jack fought for breath, gnashing at the air with bared teeth. His soul feeling the creeping death of nothingness.

The chaos halted and Jack fell to his knees. His lungs, now free, sucked in the hot desert air. His body left powerless, as if he'd just run a marathon. His muscles still short-circuiting, winding down.

The shadows around him parted and Jack could see the man standing in the breach.

"You really want to see who you are? You want to see the reward you've been earning all these years? Well, get ready, Jack . . . here it comes!"

The man's laugh echoed across the desert as the shadows swarmed over Jack in unparalleled rage. He could feel them slipping in and out of the pores of his skin, constricting his bones. He felt himself carried, twisted and contorted, into limbo, moving at breakneck speed through his own mind. Tumbling through a wormhole of desperation, clawing at his conscience in unrelenting punches to his psyche.

He could see Laura quietly weeping at home while he slept soundly in the bed next to her. He saw the old employee at work resting in a pine box on his desk in his corner office. He saw the stalled car on a deserted highway.

Visions of everything and nothing he ever did fired off from every synaptic nerve in his brain. He saw himself beating the bully from his early school days. He saw himself mourning the death of his colleague. He saw his parents mourning the death of the infant they named Jack.

His mind fought for sanity. He knew these visions made no sense, but he could do nothing to ward off the chaos. The assault on reason was too great. His hands were useless to defend against the beasts ripping at the fabric of his soul.

He screamed in agony.

He screamed for relief.

He screamed for help.

And in an instant, all was quiet as Jack floated through blackness, drifting into unconscious oblivion.

Laura opened her eyes but could not see anything. Just blackness with a shimmer of unfocused light at the peripherals.

She had come in and out of consciousness several times and her mind tried to make a narrative out of the fragments. She could feel her hands bound, and that she was on a hard surface. She tried to move her arms, but her muscles screamed in agony. She felt as if she had been in a car accident. Or beaten. That is what had happened. A beating.

Despite the pain, she forced herself into a seated position and let the blood circulate through her veins. Her head began to clear from the throbbing as she thought about what happened. She remembered swinging, clawing, thrashing against the madman. But to no avail. The initial blows had shocked her system, the subsequent ones fell on numbed nerves, and then she blanked out.

She could remember the sensation of being in the bed of the truck, jostling back and forth on a bumpy road.

Darkness.

A cave entrance.

Her eyes began to focus and she could see where she was. A cave.

Next to her lay Molly. Tied up also and unconscious. Across the room she could see Colten staring at her.

"What are you going to do with us?" Laura asked, still dazed and confused, forcing herself to stay conscious.

"Shut up!"

"Where are we?"

"I said *shut up!*"

Colten walked across the cave and slapped Laura in the face.

He was impatient. He looked at Molly and wanted fulfillment. Completion. He wanted to end the task he had halted several days before. But his hand was stayed by Seth's command.

Colten stepped outside to calm his nerves. He wouldn't be able to restrain himself if he remained in their presence, he knew that much. He was itching to get started. It was Christmas morning, but he was told he couldn't open his presents. He stewed in his own inertia.

Seth came walking up the two-track, his stature not as strong as usual, but carrying just as much venom. He resembled a kid returning from a scolding in the principal's office who then goes on to plot the means to blow up the school. He walked straight up to Colten and looked him in the eye but said nothing. Only stared deep into his heart. Colten flinched and diverted his eyes.

"What happened to you?" Seth asked.

Colten dismissed his broken nose. "Let's just say it wasn't a walk in the park."

"So, did you get her?"

Colten looked back up and smiled an evil grin. "I got more. I got the girl too."

The man did not respond with the enthusiasm that Colten had hoped for.

Colten erased the impish grin from his face and looked back to the cave. "They're in there. All that's left is to do the job."

"No, that's not all that's left."

"What do you mean?"

"Somebody's coming. Coming up here after them."

Colten looked around. "Who?"

"Jack."

Colten searched his memory.

The woman's husband. He remembered Jack vaguely like a memory easily discarded that lingers in the back of the head, refusing to be tossed aside. It came back to him.

The man who was with the woman.

The weak guy.

The one acting.

"Jack . . . ," Colten whispered. He shrugged his shoulders. "What's the big deal? He should be easy to put down."

Seth looked up. His malice, his rage, his fear burning in his eyes and staring a hole through Colten's head.

"He's not coming alone."

The spider stood in the dust, staring at the collapsed man on the ground. Jack forced his eyes open, a now common struggle that he wasn't getting used to. He could see the eight-legged demon staring him down—like the time in the car, like in the cave. This nagging creature following him around at his lowest points. A creature kicking him while he was down.

All seemed lost. He had never felt so alone.

Laura.

Her name floated through his mind. How had he come so far without realizing that he needed her? She was his strength. The one person who would have been by his side if he had just noticed.

We become immune to the sweet smell of beauty when it walks daily in our ordinary lives, but once removed, the pain of its loss is irreplaceable.

How he wanted her there with him. To hold her. To tell her that she meant everything to him. To tell her that he was wrong. That he had invested in all the wrong things. That she deserved better than what she got. But it was too late. She was gone. And so was he.

Jack stared at the spider but did not care anymore. The bug could come over and devour him and he wouldn't resist. He had no strength in his soul to think of himself as a warrior. A façade he had built up. It was now demolished.

He was nothing. She had been everything.

"I'm sorry . . . Laura," he whispered.

A shadow passed over his face, temporarily blocking the sun, and a boot came crashing down on the spider. Its eight little legs spasmed at the blow, its body turned to mush. Then, a flood of cold water washed over Jack's body and all his senses came alive. He gasped in shock.

Strength returned to his arms, and he pushed himself up. He wasn't dead . . . though he wished he were. No, he was still here, clinging to this mortal coil. He looked up into the sun and saw *him*, standing over him with an empty bucket, chew dripping down his beard and a grin on his dirty face.

"You done sleeping?"

Boots. He was alive.

"But . . . I . . . killed . . ." Jack struggled to get up.

"Takes more than that, Jack. You think I ain't been struck before?"

The old man threw down the bucket and walked over to a stool. He sat down and rubbed his side. He looked no worse for wear, like the shovel that Jack had unleashed on him made no effect in dimming his dingy exterior. The man before him made no sense to Jack. He had seen him, dead to rights, flat on the ground.

"But I saw you. You were . . ."

"Naw . . . I've gotten it worse than that. You'd be surprised what some people can think up to throw at you."

"Who are you, Boots?"

The old man hesitated. Thinking, searching. "Doesn't much matter, does it, Jack? Point is . . . you're finding out who you are. And by judging it . . . you can swing a shovel, for starters." Boots laughed at his own joke, the way he always did, and crossed his leg, rocking back and forth on his stool. "Naw . . . I ain't so much a mystery. I'm what people think of me. At least in their minds. Crazy, mean, useless . . . don't really much matter though. I am who I am."

"Is Laura dead?"

Jack waited for the answer. All his reason told him she was. He had convinced himself of that. But his heart in its newfound rhythm sang to him a song of hope.

"She ain't dead, Jack."

Elation poured over his body and tears came to his eyes. Jack began to shake, releasing himself to his feelings for her.

"But she ain't in a good spot either. Her or Molly. Naw . . . the way I see it, they're going to need you right about now."

"What do you mean? What are you saying, Boots?"

The old man stood and put his hand on Jack's shoulder. The fleshy mitt felt warm through his shirt. Vibrant. Strengthening.

"I'm sayin', Jack . . . you think you're ready to get your life back?"

PART FOUR

THE MOUNTAIN

They started into the west as fast as the horse could carry them. The poor beast had gotten a workout the past twelve hours, but she poured her heart into carrying the riders through the sagebrush. Her hoofbeats drummed a driving rhythm, a staccato that matched Boots's whip of the reins and Jack's pounding heart.

They reached the base of the mountains in no time at all, as if the horse had sprouted wings and flown. Once to the base, they headed south, the shadows fully encasing them as dusk settled across the land. Jack's thoughts were solely on Laura, as if he had turned into a knight from the round table, galloping toward a castle tower for his princess. But though the scene smacked of old-school chivalry, the fear welling up in his stomach scared the life out of him.

For all the daydreams of laying the wood down on people who ticked him off, he had never been in a fight. Had never thrown a punch, save for the swing of the shovel at an old desert hermit not more than an hour ago. He didn't know what to do. All he knew was that Laura and Molly were in trouble and he had to do something to save them.

Boots had grabbed the shotgun and slung it in a sleeve attached to the saddle horn. Perhaps Jack would just follow the old man up to wherever Laura was and let him do the talking, the bullying. It was the only thing in this whole chaotic mess that brought him comfort. Somehow, Boots seemed like he had this under control. Best to rely on him—a thought that Jack still could not believe was racing through his mind.

The slope to their right slowly subsided, and Jack could see a worn depression running across their path that headed up the mountain. A two-track. The entrance to Mordor. Boots pulled back on the reins and the horse came to a grateful stop. They got off and Boots patted the mare, thanking her for her good work.

"We walk from here."

Jack looked up at the winding path, walled in on both sides, as it snaked upward out of sight into the increasing blackness. Once on that road, anything coming up or down would plow right into them. There was no escapé exit on either side. Boots sensed the apprehension in Jack and stepped up next to him.

"What are you waiting for, Jack? Laura is up that road. No use wasting time."

Boots started walking up the trail without hesitation. Jack followed, his bravery razor thin as he forced one foot in front of the other. Once inside the mountain walls, he looked behind. The desert floor stretched out to the horizon behind him. He wondered if it would be the last time he would see it. A photograph of emptiness forever etched into his mind. Turning his back on the entrance, he looked up at Boots, who was standing a few yards ahead. The old man didn't say anything, no biting jab for this singular moment. Instead, he gave him a look of weathered reassurance.

The walls seemed to be moving in on him, their mottled jaggedness resembling an animal's jaw ready to devour him whole. The rock appeared to feed on his trepidation. But Laura was up there, somewhere past the winding bends and the dark.

The vision of Laura in the car, baking in the heat, her life ebbing away from her, returned to him full force. He could not do anything then. He could not save her from the highway and his foolishness. Now, he could do just that. Now he could become something she needed.

"Come on, Jack," Boots whispered in a voice he had not used before.

Is it the actual blow that causes so much suffering, or the anticipation of it? The waiting for the strike of pain that we know is coming and every fiber in our body tenses in macabre expectation. The road before him was the physical embodiment of the question. He could not will himself to the end of the story; he had to walk the gauntlet of fear.

And with nothing but guts and faith in Boots, Jack stepped, and stepped again, slowly up the mountain to whatever fate was in store for him. He did not look back again but trained his gaze forward on the rock, the trail, and the slow swaying of Boots's awkward cadence.

Red sat in his little office with the breeze of an oscillating fan blowing across his face and ruffling the pages on his desk. After leaving the gas station, he drove over to PJ's parents' place. The local minister had gone over as a favor to Red and broke the news. He didn't know how to do it, but in the daylight he felt it was not only his duty but a need to go. A way to grieve openly with those who would grieve too. It had worked. They all cried like babies in each other's arms.

Now he sat in the dark. The fading light of sunset breaking through the slats in the venetian blinds. A bottle of bourbon sat close by with a full, unsipped tumbler close at hand. He hadn't drunk since his wife died ten years ago from a heart attack while walking their dog. Another inexplicable, unnecessary death. It took him a couple years to come to terms and lose the booze. But now he just wanted some easy comfort.

He could see Officer Morey coming in through the front door of the station for her first day of work. She was overly excited for such a dull assignment, as if anything exciting ever happened out this way. But she brought with her a breath of fresh air. Before, it had just been him and James, and the occasional local posse that formed when someone's kid had wandered off. Now she was gone, and it would be back to just him and James wasting the hours for the next twenty years.

Red did his best to rationalize, to reason. But he fell short. He remembered sitting with his mother when bad things happened as a child, and she would say, "All things happen for a reason." The same woman sat with him at the funeral of his wife, looked at him, and said the same stupid thing. He wanted to slap the words out of her mouth. Sitting now in the twilight, staring down a bottle of whiskey, he could hear those words as if they were on a recorded loop in his head.

What reason could there be for a young vibrant cop to get smashed to bits on a road, left to die alone in such a barbaric way? If there was a reason, a great plan mapped out, then the writer of the script was simply a sick, twisted sadist.

The front door of the station opened and James walked in. He took off his cowboy hat and wiped his head off, showing the sweat stains in his pits that had soaked through his shirt. It had been a long day.

"Hey, Red."

"James."

James looked at his boss and the bottle. He didn't attempt to say anything. Every man has to wrestle with his own demons. Hat in hand, he let Red know what he found out.

"I think I got something, Red. Not too many people in town know too much, 'cept that Cole runs the gas station. But I ran into Mrs. Kennedy over at Gladys's, and she said she remembered seeing Cole up beyond Mule Deer just last week. Said she tried to wave to him, but he just sped on past. Don't remember much else after that though."

"Mule Deer?"

"Ain't much up there."

Red sat back in his chair thinking it over. "All right. Why don't you go home and get some sleep. You look whipped."

James turned to head out, but then stopped. He looked as if he had just broken his mother's china and was attempting to confess. "Don't know if I'll be able to though. I just keep seeing her . . . I can't get it out my mind."

"You okay, James?"

"Yeah . . . I think so, Red. It's just . . . I don't know . . ."

"I know, son, just go home and try to clear your mind."

James glanced back at Red, the bottle of bourbon, and then back to the floor.

"All right, boss," he said as he left.

The emptiness of the station suddenly became apparent to Red and he got up out of his chair. He grabbed the glass of whiskey and slowly poured it back in the bottle. He wouldn't drink tonight; he didn't want to start down that road. He tucked the bottle into the bottom drawer of the desk for the time he knew he would change his mind.

He left the station and started to drive north, the headlights still not competing with what sun was left. He looked out the open driver's window to the mountains now stripped of their color by shadows. Maybe Cole was up there, hiding from the awful thing he did. Or maybe he was on his way to Mexico. Who knew?

Why couldn't it have been Cole who killed PJ? Sure, he had seen him every couple days when he stopped in to the store to grab a drink. They had made small talk each time. Weather . . . mostly just weather.

"You can't much know someone when that's all you talk about," Red said to himself as he recalled his stops there, trying to find a clue. The majority of the people in Goodwell didn't know Colten either. Most knew him like Red did, as the guy who would take their money after they had pumped their gas. A simple "thanks" would be the extent of what many ever said to the man. The few who thought they knew Cole steered clear of him, something in their gut telling them that he was no good.

Red drove, aimless. He didn't want to go home and sit in front of the TV set and mindlessly burn away the hours.

He found himself coming up to the road, and eventually the spot where he was last night. He parked the car and stepped out. The wreckage was gone, towed back to Goodwell. The ambulance had taken what was left of Officer PJ away quietly, its lights off and silent.

Red squatted down and looked at the darker shade of asphalt where she had bled out her life. It would take a good rain to wipe the slate, to erase the physical memory from the road. He wished he would have brought some water to scrub the pavement, a small symbolic act of kindness. A washing away of brutality.

A light westerly wind blew across his face, bringing with it the faint scent of moisture. He looked up and could see the early signs of thunderheads forming over the mountain peaks. Somewhere up on top of the world, a storm was brewing.

"There was this man, ways back, a lot like you, Jack. He had life figured out real well. Had all the fixings you need to scratch a living. Well, one day, he got the notion in his skull to go get some more out in California. So he builds himself this huge wagon, 'cause you know, a man like that can't just travel like normal folk.

"Anyway, he stuffed his whole family in there and headed out west. Slow goin' for a long time. Passed just below Utah. Time kept wearing on them, and winter was coming.

"Folks in the train started getting antsy and second-guessing each other. Tempers got hot. They always do when things go bad. Folks get downright mean.

"One day, that man got into a fight with someone he'd been riding with. Ended up killing him dead before he knew what had happened. City man, clean hands, now finding himself standing over a dead body. Something he never reckoned he'd ever do. He couldn't imagine at what he'd just done.

"As you can reckon, folks don't get too comforted with having a murderer around them. Naw, they prefer their killers pushed out away from sight. So they all got around and tried to decide what to do with him. Some said to kill him, some said turn him out.

"Folks who said 'turn him out' won over. So they put him on a horse and made him ride out. No food. No gun. Out in wild country. They thought it'd be the easy way to kill him. He'd end up dead, but they wouldn't have to do it themselves.

"Can you think what went through his mind, having to leave behind his wife and kids in the wilderness, winter comin' on and still a long way from where they were going? He knew he was a goner, but then he must've known they were goners too."

They kept walking, Boots talking, Jack listening, up the mountain.

"That man was strong, however. Most would have given up at that point. Not him. That's the time that stubbornness comes in handy. He refused to give up the ghost. He made his way on his own to California. Alive. Then he waited out there for his family to come. They never did.

"Waiting. The misery of waiting. It can tear a man up."

The crunching of rocks below their feet beat a rhythm to Boots's story. Up the mountain.

"Then one day, word gets to him that his kin are still alive, but stuck in a mountain pass in the dead of winter. Stuck in a place that got turned to all kinds of evil."

Boots stopped, and straightened his back. He looked up the two-track as if looking through time.

"Some of the worst things swept through that pass. Folks turning savage. Not human."

Boots resumed the upward trudge.

"Anyway, that man hears that they are up there. So he goes back for them. Pushing through snow and cold. He finds them all and brings them home.

"Man had everything, lost it all, then he guts it out and gets it back. Not all, but what mattered most is what he saved. All it took was a little beatdown to set him straight.

"You may not like me, Jack. You may hate me. It doesn't matter. What matters is, are you goin' to go up there and get back what matters most?

"Not too many folks get a chance like this. To prove themselves.

But it was what you always wanted, ain't it. Wanted to show what you're made of? Well, here you go. Served up on a stick for you."

Jack watched his feet, his legs beginning to burn from the climb. He had the vague feeling of a man being marched to the gallows.

Halfway up the ascent, a small foot trail broke off to the left, and Boots stopped and sat on a rock. Jack came up a couple paces behind, bent over, and put his hands on his knees. This uphill slog was torture, his legs were burning, and sweat was pouring out of his pores. Boots looked little affected as he reached into his satchel and handed Jack some water. He drank it down in several gulps, feeling ashamed that he didn't ask if Boots needed some. By the looks of it, he didn't.

"How much farther?"

"Not too much. Just about a half mile more," Boots said, taking the container back and closing his bag. He stood up and pointed up the two-track. "A couple more turns and the road ends in a clearing. On the other side, there is a cave. They're in there. Both of 'em."

Boots stretched his back, and then started up the foot path, away from the road. Jack started after him.

"What're you doing, Jack?"

"Following you."

"Naw . . . your road's right there. That's the path you're supposed to take."

Jack looked back at the road, surprised.

Alone. He was being told to go alone.

"But . . . where are you going, Boots?"

"I got my own business needs tending."

Lost, his head swimming. Jack was paralyzed. He took a couple steps back but couldn't get himself to start the climb up the two-track. Apprehension filled his body and rooted his feet in place.

"It'll be all right, Jack. You can do this. Just head up that road and get Laura. Whatever gets in your way . . . you take it down."

Easy advice from someone going the other way, thought Jack. It made absolutely no sense to him. The old man had taken him this far, knew exactly what road to take, where Laura and Molly were; he even had a shotgun in his hand, all the keys to save them right and quick. But now he was leaving Jack just when he could have been of some use.

Running away. Just like he ran away to his shack in the desert. All talk and no muscle. All back-country wisdom and no action.

Jack looked at the gun in Boots's hand, imploring the old man to hand it over with his eyes. Boots slung it over his shoulder in response.

"Naw, Jack, you don't need this. You'd probably shoot your hand off . . . or kill one of them girls by mistake. Nope . . . you need to just march up that hill and take back what's yours. Simple as that."

And with that, Boots headed up the twisting foot trail and out of sight. He didn't look back, but his voice boomed down from above, "Now get going, Jack!"

Jack started slowly up the two-track, the way ahead now surrendering to nightfall.

His mind thumped with the crunching footsteps of his wasted legs. Up the road, he half expected to see headlights appear and charge at him, running him over after he had come this far. Or a boulder, rolling down like a Mayan booby trap. The thought of Laura up there kept him going.

He could not remember a time where he was more focused on her. No clutter. No waiting BlackBerry or office politics. All was shoved aside. It was all about her. That is what kept his legs moving, though they burned with an intensity that he had not felt since his high school sports days. It was thoughts of her that pushed the questions away, the arguments on why Boots wasn't here. It didn't matter, he told himself. The only thing that mattered now was getting up to the end of this road and saving Laura.

The twilight haze made the surrounding rock glow, as if walking into a negative photograph. Color was gone. All was doused in a sepia tinge of dark and light. The white road below his feet an unmistakable path.

Another sharp bend and Jack saw the clearing. He stopped in his tracks and hugged the rock, peering around the corner.

In the middle of the clearing was the black pickup truck. It sat there like a slumbering mythological beast, a sleeping dragon. He half expected it to turn its grill at him and charge like a chained dog, but in the increasing moonlight, it created a black hole of rusting metal.

Behind the truck, Jack could see a cleft in the rock wall. The cave. Its gaping mouth silent. Nothing stirred. It was dead quiet.

Jack thought about what to do. It was about twenty yards to the truck, possibly another twenty past that to the cave. The clearing was smooth, with no place to hide. Rock walls lined the clearing as if a scoop of earth had been lifted from the mountain. The blood pressure in Jack's veins built like a volcano.

He took a step forward and was about to make a dash for the truck when he saw a thin stream of smoke appear from behind the cab. He stepped back.

Jack could see the amber glow of a cigarette butt dancing in the dusk. A man was there, leaned up against the vehicle, facing the cave. The man inhaled again and blew the smoke into a giant ball over his head, which then dissipated in the stale air. Jack watched him cautiously. He was stuck.

Charging across the clearing, yelling like Rambo, was not the thing to do. The guy could have a gun, a knife, a bazooka, for all he knew. For a man who had never been in a fight, Jack knew enough. A cavalry charge was not his best option. He waited patiently for something to develop.

Soon the man flicked his cigarette aside and walked into the cave. Jack waited several seconds and then stepped out into the clearing.

The sound of each step seemed amplified in his ears. The crunching gravel below his shoes seemed to be screaming out with every footfall. He made his way to the truck and crouched down. Halfway there.

Halfway to what, though?

He took a peek around the tailgate and could see the cave. Darkness started just a few feet from its entrance. He could not see inside.

The tailgate. Smashed and bloody. It caught Jack's attention in the fading light as he pressed himself against the back quarter panel of the vehicle. So close to the instrument of two killings not so long ago.

Jack sat there, not knowing what to do next.

"How are we going to get out of here?" Molly's voice shook. A plea for Laura to give a reassuring answer that would somehow be prophetic.

"I don't know," Laura whispered.

In the safety of the cabin, Molly had finally told Laura about this madman. Now Laura could feel the terror in the girl as Molly was anticipating what was coming. She had been here, had seen it before. She had stared into Colten's eyes as he'd gripped her neck. She knew the evil that hung behind his pupils. The absolute insanity of bloodlust. She knew, deep down inside, that it was coming again. And by proxy, Laura knew it too. She searched for a grain of hope.

"This is it?" Molly asked.

"No."

"No?"

"No," Laura said with quiet reassurance.

They heard footsteps come through the entrance and Colten appeared, his features illuminated by the small gas lamp he had affixed to the wall, making the place seem like a mining tunnel. His face more sinister, evil in the shadow light. He looked impatient. Fidgety.

Laura could feel Molly trembling next to her as he stared at them.

"You think you two are busting out of here?"

The silence.

Colten leaned against the wall, striking a demonic James Dean pose. "Huh . . . you might as well accept it. You're already dead. Just a matter of the details."

A whimper escaped Laura's bruised lips. Molly was nearly catatonic, rocking back and forth.

"Yeah. The way I see it, this is going to be a good show. Never thought it would end this good. No way."

Colten lit another smoke, then continued on. "So tell me about *Jack*."

Laura's heart surged at the sound of her husband's name. She remained silent.

"Oh come on . . . got to be something worth talking about."

"There's nothing for us to talk about."

"Hmmm . . . I think I would agree with you. From what I remember, he wasn't much of anything. Kinda weak."

"He's a better man than you," she whispered.

"What's that?"

"I said, he's a better man than you."

Colten rubbed the back of his neck with his broken hand. Laura held her breath, willing his hair to catch fire from the cigarette still tucked between his fingers.

"Yeah, maybe so," he said. "I sure wouldn't come up here after you. All broken up. Naw, I'd leave you up here and be on my way to Vegas. You sure that isn't what he's done? Go off and leave you?"

Laura thought of Jack. Of the seeds of detachment nurtured and sprouted through the years of careful carelessness. Of the feeling she had had when she woke up yesterday to an empty bed. No letter. No note. No word. In her mind, though, she could not believe that he had abandoned her. In her hopes, he had gone to get help, in his own misguided way.

"He went for help."

"Sure he did."

"And they'll get back, and they'll find us."

Colten laughed. "You think so? What, you marry Superman or something?"

Another slow drag on the cigarette.

"Naw, it's all good. I want you to keep thinking that. Keep hoping. Keep hoping that you have a hero coming to save you. That's what makes this good. Makes it worthwhile."

He pointed over to Molly.

"See her? No hope left. Ain't going to be as good as it could've been. But you—" the smoke seeped from the corners of his mouth— "you are going to be all right. Yeah . . . you keep hoping."

His head twitched as if coming out of a trance.

"So . . . tell me . . . about Jack."

Silence.

"Is he like a Kung Fu man or something I should know about?"

"No," she whispered with downcast eyes.

"Guns, knives . . . some voodoo super power . . ."

"No."

"Well, dang, woman! What you keep him around for?"

She said nothing.

"You had some spunk in you. I'm going to pay you back tenfold for what you did to my hand. Got me wondering if I should kill you first . . . before Jack. Don't know if I can turn my back on you."

Laura looked up, eyes wide open.

"What do you mean, before Jack?"

Softly, the squeak of an ungreased door hinge flittered into the cave from the entrance. The sound of a truck door opening. Colten smiled, threw the butt down on the ground, and squashed it with his heel.

"Looks like somebody's come to save you," he said as he walked outside.

Boots made his way up the winding path, rounding rocks and marching up to the heavens like a monk sans the orange habit. The shotgun on his shoulder bouncing up and down with each step. His breath was even, as if this walk up the side of the mountain meant nothing to him, yet he climbed with determination. He was on his way to clear the air, to set things back in order. To do some work of his own.

He finally reached the termination of the narrow foot path. He stood on the edge of a ridge with a drop that went down several hundred feet. The ridge extended right and left, encircling the small clearing below. Dusk was born, and below, down in the circular canyon, Boots could see Jack making his way to the black pickup truck.

Storm clouds started gathering overhead, and shadows began to accumulate around the far edge of the ridge. A pale breeze blew through the old man's beard, then shot back and disappeared, as if stunned.

The man with the black shirt and pearl buttons appeared from Boots's left and walked toward him.

"So, decided to leave your trailer, eh, Boots?"

"Things need to get taken care of. The way I see it, you've overstepped your bounds this time. Now I got to make sure that it all gets put back straight."

Seth laughed, but anger filled the noises echoing off the rock walls. "I've spent a long time with this one. He hasn't been easy to keep rounded up. But what you did, taking that girl, that just took him off the reservation."

"Ain't my problem."

"Nothing's ever your problem, old man! You think you can just come in here and tinker with things when you want to? Naw, not this time, Boots. I've put too much energy into this one. Too much crafting, molding. This one is perfect. You aren't going to mess this one up for me, not this time."

"It's not for you to decide. I thought you'd get that through your head by now. Besides, you got the story all wrong. Naw . . . this ain't about your boy at all."

"What is it then? Why are you here now? Why shouldn't I just let my boys run over and throw you down this mountain?"

The shadows pulsed with adrenaline.

"'Cause you tried before and couldn't do it. I'm here right now. That's all you need to know."

Seth looked at the little desert hermit. His long beard, his worn-out clothes, his grime. His eyes went to the shotgun that Boots carried and smiled. "What's the gun for, Boots?"

"Gun ain't for you."

"Well, you should have given it to Jack. He's going to need it."

"Naw, he'll be fine without it."

"So why did you bring it? You just crazy?"

"Naw . . . but you take a man's wife . . . send him after her . . . make him fully realize that the only thing he has is his own hands"— Boots shook the gun—"and set him loose? Let me just say . . . they don't make a reservation big enough to hold the crazy that man becomes."

Jack took a peek around the tailgate and could see the cave, but nothing inside. He could see the distorted reflection of himself on the crumpled bumper. It looked like he had aged a hundred years. His face now spackled with stubble and growth, a few more weeks and he would be giving Boots a run for his money on the beard.

Jack could see clouds overhead, dark shadows of night gathering on the peaks all around him.

He wished Boots was with him. He never felt so scared and alone.

Jack crawled over to the passenger door and opened it up. There were no keys inside. He opened the glove box, hoping to find a weapon of some sort. There was nothing. He stepped up into the cab and looked in the bed of the pickup through the rear window. Again, nothing. His heart sank.

Climbing down, he closed the door. To his horror the hinge squeaked as he shut it, its metallic groaning echoing all around him. He crawled toward the back bumper again, finding safety by sitting next to the wheel well.

Jack dared another look around the truck.

He saw Colten come out of the cave at a slow walk, then stand at the opening.

Colten scanned the clearing and the truck.

"Jack! I know you're out there. Let's get this over with."

Jack's heart dropped. He looked back across the clearing to the two-track heading down the mountain. Every fiber in his body wanted to run, even though he knew he would not be able to make it. Colten would simply get in the truck and run him down. And he couldn't leave Laura behind . . . he had done that once, he wasn't going to do it again.

Steadfastness in the face of terror.

What is it that fills a man to make him hide in the foxhole or to storm the beach? To stand in the landing craft, waiting for the gate to open, knowing that death is just a step and blind luck away, and yet charge full-on amidst the exploding shells? Perhaps it is to consider oneself as the walking dead, that you've never been in charge of your own time. Clenching his fists, gathering every ounce of scattering bravery he had, and considering himself a dead man already, Jack stood up and walked around the back end of the truck. He could see Colten's eyes light up as he approached. Jack's legs started moving faster, knowing that if they stopped, his mind would convince them to run away. He charged, now at a full run. There were no speeches, no explanations, no high thoughts on the meaning of good or evil. Jack simply bum-rushed Colten, driving all his weight into the killer and smashing him against the rock wall next to the cave entrance.

Colten's legs buckled under him from the blow and he fell to the ground. Adrenaline flowed through Jack's body. He raised his fist and drove it across Colten's face, driving his rage into that one punch. Jack could feel his knuckles pop and pain shoot through his hand. Colten slumped, his already-broken nose exploding fresh blood, the pain knocking him out.

Jack was stunned. In less than five seconds he had dropped Colten. He looked around, not knowing what to do with the guy lying on the ground, but wanting to search for Laura. There was nothing to tie him up with. Jack searched Colten's pockets and pulled out a small key ring.

Salvation.

With Colten dispatched, Jack walked into the cave slowly.

Several steps in, he could see a dull light coming around a slight bend. He stepped up and saw the stone room illuminated by the small gas lamp. Across the room, he saw Laura and Molly.

Jack ran and wrapped his arms around his wife.

Laura hugged him back, crying in disbelief, shocked that he was actually there. Molly couldn't hold her excitement as she screamed at his entry.

Laura then pushed him back and slapped him across the face, staring into his eyes with anger, with hurtfulness. She was allowed that, he thought, she was allowed a great many things. Her fury subsided and she grabbed his shirt with both hands and buried her head in his chest. She sobbed on.

She cried out the years of frustration, of loss. She cried out the panic of the last several hours. She let loose the feelings of detachment, as if purging her soul of all the things that buried her heart.

"I don't believe this . . . ," Laura cried. "I thought you were gone."

"I know."

"I hate you."

"No . . . you don't."

She gained her composure and looked at Jack.

"No . . . I don't."

He kissed her deeply. Kissed her without reservation. A kiss to make up for not kissing her like this for too long.

He was dirty. He stunk like something fierce. His eyes were crazed as he fingered the key ring, looking for the lock to unbind the ankle shackles. He was trembling, and his knuckles on his right hand were swollen and bleeding. Laura had never seen him like this before. At that moment, she thought he was completely beautiful.

"How did you find us? How did you—"

"How about we just get out of here?" Jack said with a smile.

He worked Laura's chain until it gave way. Then he did the same for Molly.

They threw the shackles aside and stepped to the mouth of the cave, Jack leading the way with Laura right behind him. They walked into the darkness away from the lighted room. A few feet from the entrance they stopped.

Colten wasn't there.

Red continued north along the highway when something in the dimming light caught his attention on the side of the road. He stopped the car and got out. Crossing the pavement to the western side, he knelt down and looked at the dirt leading off. There was a large tire track, turning slightly south toward Goodwell as it terminated in the asphalt. He looked up toward the mountains and could see it, like a '90s holograph painting, the scene coming into view once you have lost focus. Red could see it.

A two-track heading west toward the mountains. And in the mountain, a gap, probably the space where the two-track kept on going. Right above the spot, he could see the storm clouds intensifying, as if the storm was directing its rage at that one solitary location. Concentrating its attention.

Red walked back to his car, started it up, and turned off the road, headed up the two-track. It seemed pointless, but what else was he going to do tonight. He couldn't go home and think about PJ anymore. He didn't want to sit alone in the dark where the temptation of the whiskey could sneak up on him. Better to keep driving, even if it was into the wasteland as night fell.

It was several miles of rough driving, the suspension on the car yelling in agony. This was not the vehicle for the job. Red's back began to complain, but he adjusted himself in the seat and drove on, the glow of the dash lights illuminating his face in the ever-increasing dark.

He clicked on his windshield wipers, temporarily blinded as the dust and bugs turned to mud in the sprinkle coming down. The headlights cutting two swaths of white down the brush-covered road.

It took a long time, but he finally made it to the mountain base. He put it in park and got out. The rain was increasing, but he ignored it. Water dripped from the brim of his cowboy hat, encasing his head in a slow waterfall. His shirt began clinging to his back. Red took the flashlight from his belt and pointed it at the mountain as he walked closer.

He could see that the two-track kept going, winding up the mountain out of view. The rock walls looming on each side. It was pointless, he thought to himself. Driving all the way out here for no reason. But something in his gut was pulling him forward, that inkling at the back of his neck that told him he should keep going.

Red turned around and got back into the car. He sat there for a moment, contemplating the road ahead.

He put the car in drive and eased into the chasm.

It fit, like a snake unhinging its jaw to swallow a rat.

He started up the winding staircase, the headlights painting macabre shadows on the rocks before him. He could hear the patter of the rain on the metal hood of the cruiser and the echo of the engine humming as he drove up to the sky.

The shadows began to dance on the top of the mountain. Some becoming brave enough to whisk by the old man but not daring to touch him. Hurling silent insults at Boots, trying to provoke him. He stood calm. Unaffected.

Boots had looked approvingly from above as Jack laid out Colten and ran inside the cave. Seth's anger began to build, reflected in the increasing storm overhead. The rain came down and pelted the hermit's clothes like tiny fists. Boots was soon soaked, the water running off his beard in strands, dripping onto the ground before him. A shaggy dog in a waterfall.

"Is that who you're putting your money on, Boots? Really? He doesn't stand a chance, and you know it."

Boots looked down into the chasm as if gazing into a cauldron. The scenes of the fight coming up to him in prophetic bubbles.

"Sure was cruel of you, old man. Bringing a guy like that out here. Even I couldn't think that one up. And you think I'm the depraved one!"

"It ain't over, Seth. Don't you go getting ahead of yourself."

Seth laughed . . . the thunder rolling through the clouds. "You're sick. Old and sick in the head. You know what the worst thing is . . . you probably told him that he had a chance. That he could come up here and get back down the mountain in one piece. Didn't you?"

"You best shut your mouth . . . it'll be the last time I tell you."

"Or what? What're you going to do, Boots? You going to curse me? No . . . you are just going to slink back to your edge of the world and hide out for the rest of time, pouting about the way things are. You never had the nerve to stick around, to finish what you started. To see the potential in this place. No, you're not going to do anything. Just like that time up in Reno—yeah, you're not going to do anything."

Boots pulled back his arm and swung, backhanding the air in front of him. A ripple of force shot out, knocking the shadows on the far canyon wall into oblivion. The remaining shadows looking on stunned, shocked.

"Not this time, Seth. Naw, I think I'm goin' to stick around for a bit. Get my hands dirty this time."

Gradually, like slow-boiling oil over a Norse campfire, the fury in Seth built up, spilling over into his shadowy cohorts surrounding the ridge. He screamed, unleashing a torrent of wind, thunder, and lightning that filled the sky and echoed out across the desert to the east like a sonic boom.

Boots found himself surrounded by shadows taunting him on all sides, each one waiting for its neighbor to have the stomach to take the first swing. The hermit stood firm, the rain pouring down his face, his eyes narrowed, the crow's feet ready to claw out his cheeks. A faint smile crossed his lips.

"Now, old man . . . you are going to wish you never came up here," Seth yelled.

Calm filled the air around Boots, as if the world inhaled before diving into deep water.

"Naw . . . now you're going to see who you've been messing with."

And with those words, all hell broke loose.

72

They watched the rain pour down from the mouth of the cave opening. Jack scanned the clearing, but apart from the truck, nothing was there. He tried to think of a plan as fear began to replace the adrenaline coursing through his blood.

"What are we going to do?" Laura asked, waiting for Jack to move.

Jack thumbed the key ring in his hand. "We make for the truck. Quietly. One of these keys has to work on it."

"All right."

"No hesitation now."

"All right."

Jack led the way, the puddles forming in the clearing slapping under his feet. He got to the driver's door and opened it. He pushed Laura and Molly in and he got inside, slamming the door shut behind him.

"Get the locks!" he said to Laura as he tried the key he had selected in the cave. No luck.

He tried another one.

Then a third.

The girls were huddled in the passenger seat, soaking wet, but shaking more from fear than from the water.

"Which one is it?" Jack yelled in frustration.

Lightning flashed.

Jack could not see the shadow standing in the truck bed, illuminated by the quick flash.

All he heard was the sound of breaking glass as Colten's boot kicked the rear window open. The glass shattered into the truck cab, and Jack's head hit the steering wheel. Colten reached into the truck, the thick chain in his hands, and wrapped it around Jack's neck. He looked at Laura and Molly.

"I'll be right back," he sneered.

Then with a pull, he yanked Jack through the back window and into the truck bed. Jack could feel glass shards scrape his back, shooting pain down his spine. The rain and darkness blinded him as he lay face up, being dragged by his neck off the truck and onto the clearing floor.

Colten released the chain and took a few steps back. The lightning illuminating his face with each crash. Blood streamed down his face from his twice-broken nose. Hell was in his eyes. Jack could see the swinging chain in the madman's hand.

"You got guts, Jack. More than I thought you had."

Jack rolled and tried to get to his feet, when he felt the chain hit his face. It was pain like he had never felt before. The enormity of it knocked him backward and he hit the ground hard, the wind leaving his chest like a soul leaving a body. He could feel his face swelling up, his heartbeat thumping in his cheeks, as the tears rolled from his eyes uncontrollably. He didn't want to get up. Didn't want to feel any more pain like that. Then he heard Colten yell.

"You two get back in that truck! You hear! Get back!"

Jack forced himself up. His head pounding. He couldn't tell if his face was pouring blood or if it was just the rain. He saw Laura backing away from Colten slowly, Molly hiding behind her. Colten was swinging the chain like a train conductor with his watch.

Laura saw Jack rising, Colten turning to follow her eyes. He smiled when he saw Jack.

"You getting up? You sure about that, Jack?"

Jack looked at Laura. "Run!"

She didn't hesitate. Laura grabbed Molly's hand and sprinted down the two-track out of the clearing. Colten looked back at the girls and yelled, but before he could react, Jack crashed into his back with the force of a charging lion.

The two fell to the ground, sending blood and mud flying.

Jack tried to pin Colten down, but took a fist to the face that sent him rolling off the madman. He quickly regained his feet this time and ran to the back of the truck, looking for anything he could use as a weapon. It was then that he felt the incredible sting of the chain break against his hip.

Jack's legs buckled as he fell to his knees, his hands still gripping the tailgate. He saw the chain come down on his fingers, and he screamed as his weight dropped from the truck. He looked up and could see Colten again, staring down at him.

"I can do this all day, Jack, if you wanna!"

Colten squatted next to Jack and spit in his face. He knelt there, looking over his prey. "You got to get it through your head. I ain't got nothing to lose. As soon as I'm done with you, I'm simply going to go down and get those two and bring 'em back. Take my time with them. Especially Laura. Yeah, she is a feisty one. A lot of grit in her. She going to be fun." Colten licked his lower lip and sucked in his cheeks. He spit again, blood mixing with his saliva. "Yeah, she going to be real nice."

Jack's mind raced . . . a thousand images a second. The script from the week before ran through his mind, making its way through the agony in his body, pushing its way through the crowd to the front of the stage.

Always back to the head slam to the counter. Yes, the head slam would definitely be the way to go . . .

Jack felt the adrenaline return to his body, the rage, the fire. He reached up with both hands and grabbed the back of Colten's neck. With all his strength, he slammed Colten's head into the smashed truck bumper. He held nothing back. No reservation.

Colten screamed. His broken nose spewing forth fresh blood. His eyes welling shut from the misery of splintered bone and flesh. The murderer buckled under the pain, dropping the chain as he put his hands to his face.

Jack rolled to his feet again and grabbed the chain. He swung it back and, with everything he could muster, brought it down on Colten's back.

The storm raged over head. Shadows flew in sweeping arcs, dive-bombing the old man who stood undaunted. Seth directed his energy like an enraged Mozart, flinging his malice at Boots with all the anger of the centuries. With each passing second, Seth's hatred grew until it consumed him, burning in his eyes and animating his limbs.

Boots deflected each passing wave with the agility of a dancer. His grizzled hands grasping at shades and squeezing them out of existence. He was at the eye, the center of the storm. The focus of the dark whirlpool's rotation. With one eye he kept a watch over Jack below, with the other, he waged war with the mist.

The rain came down sideways, the whole world illuminated by the spiderweb lightning stretched out across the black sky. Boots moved his feet and marched up to Seth, grabbed him by the neck, and brought him to the ground. His iron grip as old as the rock beneath his feet.

The shadows swarmed impotently around him, on his back, over his arms. They fought to tear the old man away from their master but could not. He was locked in . . . immovable.

Seth grinned back at Boots, unfazed by the quick turn of events. His laugh resounded in the echoing booms of the lightning strikes.

Laura ran blindly down the two-track, pulling Molly behind her. The rain slapped their faces as they picked up steam, the incline almost sending them tumbling forward.

How could she leave Jack back there?

She cried, she screamed, she ran.

Into the blackness, their feet crunching in the rock, they continued their downward spiral, expecting the pickup truck to come barreling after them. Laura didn't know what to do. She had to find help. Find Boots. Find someone to go up and save Jack.

Suddenly they saw lights flash from down below them. Headlights coming around the next twist in the road. They were blocked in, nowhere to hide. Laura pressed Molly against the wall, the young girl in the woman's embrace. They didn't know who was coming, what was coming.

The car came into view and stopped, its headlights full on the two scared souls. With much scraping and pushing, the driver's door opened and they could see a man get out. He walked to the front of the car and stood before the headlights, his shadow casting a large impression on the stone behind them.

"You girls all right? What are you doing up here?"

"Who are you?" Laura screamed, hysterical.

"Easy now, missy. I'm the sheriff around here."

Red approached the woman and the young girl. He could see bruises on the woman's face come into view as he got closer. "What's going on? Now you tell me."

The woman moved and ran over to Red. She collapsed on him in relief, crying, disoriented. She could not talk fast enough as she tried to explain the whole situation at once. He listened, studying both of them closely.

"You have to help him, he's still up there!"

"Who's up there?"

"Jack! My husband! Please!"

"Did he do this to you?"

"No . . . it was Colten . . . a man named Colten!"

Red's blood began pumping hot. "You said Colten's up there?"

"Yes!"

"All right. You two keep walking down. Careful now," he said as he handed them the flashlight from its holster. "I'll get this taken care of."

He ushered the women around the car and saw them off, their worried faces awash in the red taillights of the cruiser. He got back in the car and picked up the radio.

"James, you there?"

He waited.

"James, pick up if you hear me."

Again nothing.

Red put the car in drive and continued up the mountain, watching Laura and Molly disappear in his rearview mirror as he rounded the corner. He soon came to the end of the road and drove into the clearing. The rain coming down was a complete monsoon. Through the wiper blades he could make out a truck in the center, and what looked liked two people. He drove closer and got out, his hand on his revolver.

He saw Colten down on the ground, holding his face and screaming.

The other man he didn't know, but he could see that he was wielding a large chain and was about ready to bring it down on Colten's back. Red lifted his weapon and yelled.

"Drop the chain!"

Lightning boomed across the chasm, deafening the canyon with thunder.

Red saw the man bring the chain down on Colten with absolute remorselessness. Colten screamed again.

"Drop the chain!"

The man wound up again, his eyes solely latched on to his prey. The chain swung over his head, gathering steam for another blow.

Red fired his weapon.

75

The gunshot rang through the canyon, and Boots released his grip from Seth's throat. He stood up and looked at the apparition lying on the ground before him. He wanted nothing more than to drive his boot into his face and squash him like a bug. But he didn't. He restrained himself. For the sake of a feeling that Seth could never understand, the old man stayed his rage. Seth slowly stood up and dusted himself off, eyeing Boots cautiously as one unsure of his opponent's next move.

"You best be getting gone before I change my mind," Boots whispered.

The storm around him subsided, all its energy dissipating like a wounded dog scurrying out of someone's front yard. Seth took a few steps back, sizing up Boots. He looked over the side of the canyon at the scene forming below, at the cop holding the pistol, at his champion's bloodied and broken face. The fight here was winding down, and he could feel that he was on the losing side.

"All right, Boots. All right." Seth spit the venom out of his mouth. It mixed with the last of the raindrops and spilled down the stone. "I'll let you have this one. Cole was about used up anyway. No use for him no more. But look down there before you get all high and mighty. Look there, and you'll see rage boiling. Only this is better. Ain't twisted and sick. No, this pure. Justifiable. Took awhile to get there, but now it shows up. Once that gets unleashed, ain't no going back again."

The final number of shadows evacuated the ridge, off to their home on the other side of reality. Stillness fell over the top of the world.

"This is where you're supposed to say your words . . . ain't it, Seth? Something like *This ain't over* or something like that?"

"You know, Boots. You know. What's the use in saying it?"

"I know. I know there's goin' to come a time when you and me will have ourselves a reckoning. Where we're gonna get this done for. Get this good and done."

"You'll never have it in you, old man."

"I already do."

"No, Boots, you don't. You lack the will. The will to take charge. You're at your best when you're tucked away, hiding like a coward from all us boogeymen. You go on back now. Back to your trailer. Back to living alone and blaming the world for forsaking you."

"You need to wish I'll do that."

Seth laughed as he took a few more steps back. "Keep humoring yourself, old man." He spit again, then smiled an evil grin, turned, and walked away into the darkness, melting into the night.

Boots looked up at the now clear sky, the stars shining down and washing the mountain in soft radiance. He looked east across the desert valley, the stillness of the quiet wasteland. His corner of the earth.

"It was something once . . . ," he whispered to himself.

He looked down into the canyon and watched the outcome of the battle from up on high.

Alone.

Jack thought he could feel the bullet pass over his head, or in time, that is what he convinced himself. He looked up, stunned to find a cop pointing a pistol at his head.

"Drop the chain!" the man yelled at him.

He dropped the weapon to his feet and looked down at Colten. The man was beaten. His face gushing blood from his mouth, his nose.

With the fight over, the full pain came back into Jack's body and he fell too. His face felt swollen and throbbed at the rate of his slowing heart. His side felt shattered. He didn't know how he had been standing a moment before. Jack could feel his body going into shock, the stinging agony washing over him with each passing second.

Red walked up to the pair of bloodied pugilists. The rain coming to an end and clearing up with each passing footstep.

"You Jack?" he asked. "I said, are you Jack?"

Jack nodded his head, the stiffness of his neck tensing up before he knew what was happening. The cop moved his weapon and trained it on Colten, who looked up at him with blackened eyes, his head resting on the bumper of the pickup truck. Red kept the gun and his eyes on the madman, but kept talking to Jack.

"Can you get up? Can you walk?"

"I . . . I don't know."

"Well, try."

Jack attempted to stand again, but his right leg gave way with newfound pain. He fell against the tailgate and put all his weight on his left foot. Every muscle in his body screamed at him. Every nerve resisting his attempts to get up.

"I need you to go get in my car. Get in there and shut the door. I'll get you out of here soon enough."

"But . . ."

"Shut up. Get in the car and shut the door."

Jack drug himself across the clearing. The starlight now shining down and illuminating the stone floor. He cried in pain with each step . . . his strength completely gone. He made it to the car, opened the back door, and lay down on the bench seat. He wanted nothing more than to fall asleep. To pass out. To escape the pain that was now consuming every part of his body. He didn't have the will to bend his legs and shut the door like he had been ordered. He didn't care anymore.

Out in the clearing, Red waited until Jack had thrown himself into the back of the cruiser. Then he looked down at Colten, the end of his pistol fixed between his eyes.

"What are you going to do, Red?" Colten asked, fear building up inside him.

His rage had left him. Colten couldn't explain the sensation that he now felt, as if suddenly one had the feeling of breaking free from a straightjacket. He sensed that he was alone. Abandoned. Left behind enemy lines without protection. He was scared, as scared as he imagined the young girls he had brought up here must have been. But now he was on the flip side of this evil game and he didn't like it. Staring into Red's eyes, Colten tried to discern if he had that same look behind the pupils. He searched for bloodlust.

"What are you doing, Red?" he squealed.

Red looked at the back of the pickup truck. It was smashed. The kind of damage one would think a truck would have if it slammed into the front of a police cruiser. His eyes traced the lines of the dents, imagining how his young officer's body had bent the metal as it was pinned between the two vehicles. The rain had washed away the flakes of paint and any remembrance of PJ's life that may have resided on the twisted bumper.

"Please," Colten begged. "Please don't do it."

Red thought of his young officer coming through the station after one of her shifts. All smiles and full of life. He remembered every bad thing that happened to someone he cared about. He was lost in anguish, justifying what he was about to do. Convincing himself of the sweet release of judgment that he would feel by blowing away the trash of humanity crumbled on the ground before him.

Red cocked the hammer back.

"No, Red . . . no!"

"Shut up, Cole."

And with that he fired.

The bullet passed out the barrel of the gun with a blinding flash of heat and percussion. It traveled beyond sight, and tore through Colten's thigh right above his kneecap. Cole screamed in torment.

Red holstered the gun and grabbed his handcuffs. He then drug Cole to the wheel well of the pickup and chained his wrist to the spring.

"I'll be back to pick you up, Cole," Red said. "Or at least what's left of you after the coyotes are done with you."

"You can't leave me here . . . Red . . . Red!"

Red walked to his cruiser. He pushed Jack, who was passed out, all the way into the car and shut the door. He got in, fired up the engine, and backed out of the clearing. The headlights flashed across the truck as he turned, and he could see Colten one last time screaming and pulling at the chain.

Red felt a cold sense of happiness, of fulfillment, as he drove down the mountain.

PART FIVE

HOME

Jack awoke to the sounds of hospital noises. He was lying in a bed with white linen, fluorescent light shining off the chrome railings on the side of the gurney.

Laura sat next to him, holding his hand. The bruises on her face still showing. She smiled at him, her radiance restored to her.

"Hi there," she said.

"Hi."

"You going to make it?"

"I think so."

"I thought I would never see you again."

"I know."

He could hear orderlies talking outside his door. "I'm sorry I ran off."

"It's okay."

"I'm sorry for a lot of things."

"I know." She squeezed his hand. He felt pain flare up in his knuckles where the chain had come down, but he didn't tell her. He didn't want her to let go.

"I hate Las Vegas," he said.

She laughed.

He drifted back to sleep.

Red came into the hospital room sometime later. He pulled up a chair on the other side of Jack's bed and started asking questions of Laura. Jack tried to follow the conversation, but drifted in and out.

"We found your rental, miles away from any road."

"But that doesn't make any sense," she said.

"What happened?"

"The car died on a highway, nobody came."

"What highway?"

"I'm not sure, we were just off sightseeing."

"Did you walk away from the car?"

"No, Boots came and got us. He saved us. Took us back to his place."

A long pause.

"Boots?"

"Yes."

"You sure that was his name?

"Yes."

"Uh-huh."

Jack drifted into darkness again.

"Do you know where this trailer is?"

"Not really," she said.

"Can you take a guess?"

"About an hour from the cave, I would think."

"You sure about that?"

"Pretty sure. It seemed like that long from the back of the truck."

"Could you see any landmarks?"

"No."

"No?"

"I was tied up in the truck bed."

"Yes, you said that already."

Jack woke again as Red was leaving the room. The cop came back and stood next to him. His old grizzled features worn from desert living. He addressed the couple.

"You've both had quite the ride, haven't you? Well, you put up a pretty good fight, Jack. Took a lot of guts."

"Thanks," Jack said weakly, his head still spinning between dreamland and reality.

"I wouldn't recommend doing it again, taking on a killer with your bare hands, but if it was my missus up there, I'd like to think I would be able to do the same thing."

Jack thought about those words . . . "taking on a killer." He had never been as scared in his whole life as he had been walking up that mountain. He doubted whether he would ever be able to forget that feeling. The fight blurred together in a flash of blended action, but the walk, no, he would always remember that and find quiet pride inside that he had done it. Had fought against all fear, and saved Laura. It was an accomplishment to last a lifetime.

Red started to leave when Laura spoke up.

"Boots will confirm what we told you. We wouldn't be here without him."

The cop stood by the door, nodded to them, and left.

James was standing in the hallway waiting for him. He had spent the morning talking with Molly in the waiting room.

"What's the girl say?" Red asked.

"Said that Cole picked her up at a diner in Vegas. That he took her up to that cave and tied her up. Said something about a guy named Boots came up and rescued her. Took her back to his trailer. That's where she met up with these two."

"Hmm."

"So you think we should go looking for this guy?"

"Search all you want, James, but you won't find nobody out there," Red replied as he started walking down the hall.

"No? What you mean?"

Red stopped and looked back, contemplating what he was going to say next. "How long have I lived here?"

"Longer than me, Red. Almost your whole life."

"Would you say I know the area pretty well?"

271

"Better than anyone, I guess. What you getting at?"

Red took a deep breath and exhaled slowly. He walked back to James and looked him in the eye. "That's right, James. I've lived here almost my whole life. Know almost everything there is to know about this place. And trust me. There ain't no old man living out there in a trailer."

James stared back blankly as Red sauntered down the hallway and out the exit door.

On the third floor of the hospital, behind a locked door guarded by an overweight corrections officer who was busy reading the paper in a not-too-comfortable chair, lay Colten. His leg was immobilized and bandages covered most of his face. His eyes were sunk in black tar pits of bruises, his lips swollen and stitched.

He spent most of his time pulling at the leather arm restraints that held him down until his energy was gone. Once rested, he would start pulling again, convinced that with enough effort he would be able to free himself. But with each tug, the restraints would grip tighter, digging into his wrists. Torturing him.

His mind raced through his life. All the girls he had taken up to the cave. All the great times he had had.

His thoughts zeroed in on that one fateful turn of events. The second-guessing when he had his hand to Molly's throat. All this was because of that. His mess-up, his rash reaction. If he had just killed her, he would not be here. He would be sitting behind the counter at the gas station, smoking a cigarette, basking in the aura of another soul snuffed out.

But no. He had hesitated, as if some unseen hand had slapped him in the head, filling him with doubt. He hated himself more and more because of this.

Colten pulled on the straps again. More out of frustration over this thought than the idea of escaping.

"You know you can't break those, don't you?" Seth said. He was standing by the closed door. His black shirt, his jeans . . . looking no worse for wear after his encounter on top of the mountain.

Anger filled Colten when he stared at the man. "You left me! Where were you?"

"I had my own business to take care of."

Another pull on the straps. "This is your fault!"

Seth laughed. He walked over to the bed, grabbed a chair, and sat down. "My fault? Really?"

"You told me to go after that woman. In the cabin. You set me up!"

"I did no such thing."

"You knew what would happen. You knew that Red would follow her back!"

Colten thrashed in the bed. The gunshot wound in his leg burned with intense pain and he stopped.

"Calm down, Cole. You need to settle down. It's over."

"Get me out of here."

"You know I can't do that."

"Get these off me!" Colten screamed, pulling once again at the restraints.

Seth stood up. "No, Cole. Your part of this is done now. You served your purpose. You messed it up, but you still did what I needed from you."

"What do you mean?"

"You stirred the pot up. Got folks thinking they should get back in the game. Can't get things done if folk don't want to cooperate. Yeah, you did enough to get 'em riled."

"You used me? You used me!"

Seth ignored the question as he made for the door, leaving Colten shouting behind him.

"You can't leave me here!"

"Yes, I can."

"I can't go to prison! I can't sit there and wait to die!"

"Oh, you won't have to worry about that," Seth whispered, as he walked toward the door and dispersed through it.

Colten pulled yet again at the restraints. It was then that he saw it. Two black little legs reaching up to the sky over the white blanket covering his feet. They flexed, feeling the air, grabbing on to the cloth and pulling its body up. A spider, bigger than anything Cole had ever seen. He gasped, but his voice had left him.

It crawled slowly up his leg, feeling its way across crisp hospital linen. Inching closer with each stuttering heartbeat. The insect's eyes staring into Colten's, staring into him, licking its fangs. It crept on, up his thigh, his waist, onto his chest.

Colten flexed his arms, every muscle taut like Samson against the pillars of Dagon, but to no avail. The creature walked deliberately, up his neck. Its legs searching for Cole's mouth, feeling their way, following the hot breath of his gasping lungs.

He could feel it pull itself into his mouth, clawing at his teeth, digging down inside him. He could not scream, he could not move.

He could no longer be.

Columbus had never looked so good.

Molly followed her parents into the house. They had flown out to Las Vegas and been with her at the hospital and during all the police questioning. Her mom, weeping and holding on to her most of the time, her father oscillating steadily between anger and thankfulness that his daughter was safe.

The death of Colten in the hospital was treated as a blessing in disguise for most involved. Molly's parents were not too eager to hang around Vegas longer than they had to, and the quick summation of the horrible ordeal meant an equally quick trip back home.

Home. A word that Molly let drift through her mind like dust in a sunbeam.

The stillness and familiarity came back to her. She had been gone only a month, but it seemed like a lifetime. Everything she had seen, everything that she had been through had changed her. It would be impossible to believe that it couldn't.

She tiptoed quietly like a tourist through her childhood memories. A time of innocence forever lost, never to be regained, a feeling of ease and peace that she had walked away from all too easily.

Regret is the heart breaking over abandoned comforts.

Molly opened the door to her room. Everything was in place, but she looked at her things with changed eyes. The bedspread that she would lie on and text with her friends about stupid things. The posters of teen idols who now seemed all but trivial. She observed herself as if a stranger.

"You all right, hon?" her mom asked, coming up behind her and hugging her again. Smothering, but welcome.

"I don't know."

"It's going to be okay. Just going to take awhile. You've been through a lot."

"I never thought I would be home again." Tears drifted down her cheeks. "I just wanted to be home so bad."

"I know."

"I'm sorry, Mom."

Molly wept, expelling all the fear and loneliness of her experience. Making room. They held each other, mother and child, no longer alone.

"Every time I close my eyes, I still see him. I know he's dead, but I still see him."

"Then we'll stay awake, me and you."

"Forever?"

"Forever."

Jack stepped off the plane with the aid of a walking stick, his new companion. The chain had done quick and dirty work to his hip bone. He sauntered up the Jetway with a limp and a grimace. The doctors assured him that the pain would subside with time, but gave less confidence that he would be able to walk without an aid going forward.

Not exactly the memento he had hoped to return with from Las Vegas.

Laura strolled beside him as they walked through O'Hare, back to the hustle and movement of Chicago life.

Home.

"Well, we're back," Jack said.

"Yeah."

"What happens in Vegas stays in Vegas, right?"

She smiled and gave him a kiss. He received it without reservation.

After the airport, they made their way home. The once lonely house now seeming a new place of hope and love.

Life settled in around them at a fast pace. Routine does that. It dulls the senses, bores a person into apathetic slumber. But the couple did their best, and when things got strained, they would talk about the desert, about the highway, about the mountain, and in the times of loneliness they would huddle back together in renewed comfort.

History. It's what they had again. A shared journey.

They would talk of Boots, sitting on his porch "out there," chewing on his tobacco and gazing at the dust and tumbleweed. They doubted they would ever see him again, and to Jack's surprise, that saddened him.

He tried to wrap his head around the mystery of it all. How their drive on that fateful day ended with them stuck on hell's highway, trapped in a trailer with a hermit, and then up a mountain to confront a homicidal maniac. It made his head hurt just trying to connect all the pieces.

Small steps of mystery.

When he'd returned to work, his colleagues asked what had happened, why he had been gone so long, why was he now walking with a cane? But as with his new method of locomotion, his bluster had been crippled too.

"Got in an accident, just glad to be home," he would say, knowing full well how incomprehensible the real story was. It was his and Laura's story, one that he would keep to himself.

Laura would have times when she thought she would see Boots in a parking lot or a crowded shopping mall. She would find herself quickening her step to catch up with the old pedestrian, only to be disappointed at finding that it wasn't him. She had a dull ache in the pit of her stomach that missed him, that had found comfort in his words and manner. At night she would dream of the front porch, the few days she had sat there with him.

The highway.

Whenever the thought of the near tragedy entered her mind, it quickly gave way to the longing of being in the company of Boots. And when she thought about the horror of the mountain, she remembered the words Boots had told her when he left to go get Jack.

"You willin' to do what it takes to get what you want? You willin' to put yourself out there to help get back what's been lost?"

Had everything been orchestrated? Had the seeming chaos been scripted? Who was Boots, really?

Whatever the answer, Laura was happy. Happy that Jack had returned to her. Not the old Jack from long ago and not the Jack of recent recollection. A Jack who had evolved into something new, grown from an experience that neither could explain but both agreed in time that it was an experience worth having.

Red drove out into the desert.

He remembered a time when he was little, sitting in his mother's prairie church. It was a funeral. He sat there fidgeting in his seat, five years old and in his brother's hand-me-down suit jacket that was still two sizes too big. The wooden pew getting more uncomfortable with each passing drone of the preacher.

The funeral was for a young man knifed in a bar fight. A son of one of his mother's friends. He remembered his mom with her arms around a weeping woman, sobbing uncontrollably. The sunbeams cutting swaths across the thick air of the sanctuary.

"It will be all right," his mother said. "There is a reason for all this."

That was what she always said. Anytime tragedy struck her orbit. Repeated words that became more meaningless with every utterance.

Red could see the day in photographic stills. Not a fluid memory, but snapshots of anguish, boredom . . . too young to grasp the full weight of what he was witnessing.

Propping himself up on his knees, he had looked to the back of the church. Through the neighbors and townsfolk. He remembered the face of an old man.

The man sat in the last pew, by himself. His weathered face

cracked like leather, his beard hanging down in front of him. Unwashed and haggard, the old man stared at Red.

The young boy stopped his fidgeting and stared back. All the other people at the service disappeared, and there was only the two. Old and young.

The man smiled with his eyes, placed his hands on the pew in front of him, and stood up. He stepped out of his seat, turned, and walked out of the church, the opening door letting the morning light rush in like a tidal wave. Red got up from his seat, and walked out behind him.

"Mister?"

The old man turned to him.

"What are you doing, mister?" Red said from the church steps.

"I'm just checking in."

"But we aren't supposed to leave until it's over. Mom says we got to wait for the preacher to say bed'iction."

The old man laughed to himself. "Is that what she says? Well, you best get back in there before she finds out. Don't want to end this day with a whipping now."

Red stood there staring. Silent.

"Is there something you want to ask me?" the old man said.

"Is there a reason for this? Mom says there's a reason."

"What do you think?"

The boy shuffled his feet, looking down as he prepared his answer. "I suppose so."

"Well, you listen to your mom. She's a good woman," he said as he turned to leave.

"Mister . . . where're you going?"

The man with the boots stopped. "Oh, don't worry. I'll be around."

And with that, he sauntered off, leaving Red on the church steps.

Through the years, he had thought of this encounter. When his wife died, and his mother was spitting out her clichés, he thought he might see that old-timer pop up again. It wasn't rational, he knew that. But Red didn't care. In his heart, he knew who the man was. The story from the couple and the runaway brought back the memory.

Red kept driving, the hardpan and rock stretching out before him. The image of the old man etched in his mind deeper than the chisel marks on an old grave marker.

And so he drove, not knowing where to go, but letting the wheel flow smoothly in his hand as if the car directed his path. The sun blazing overhead in its unending beatdown of the knocked-out desert floor. The suspension on the vehicle sweating under the constant jarring of uneven rock, sand, and brush. He drove throughout the morning, starting on the two-track that led up the mountain to where he had shot Colten, but turning north off road at the mountain's base.

He kept going, a mile past where all reason told him to turn back, his mind telling him that he was being ridiculous, that nothing was out here. He then turned the wheel east, the mountain range reflecting off the rearview mirror as the sun passed through the windshield and warmed his chest. He kept driving.

In the distance he saw the faint shimmer of a tin roof, reflecting briefly and then disappearing. Appearing again. A beacon out in the wasteland. Words, dancing in his head.

I'll be around.

Look for

SAMUEL PARKER'S

next novel that will keep you

ON THE EDGE OF YOUR SEAT.

READ THE SNEAK PEEK NOW

SPRING 2018

1

The day was born in darkness.

Michael opened his eyes and saw nothing.

Blackness.

The motes in his eyes drifted across the void.

His mouth was sealed with what felt like tape. Michael tried to lift himself and felt the hard knock of wood against his forehead. A light sprinkle of sand fell on his face, but he was blind to its source. He could only feel it as it dusted his lashes, scratching at his pupils. He raised his head slowly again until he felt the board press against his skin. He laid back down. His shoulders ached as well as his back. He tried to move his hands up to his eyes to rub the grit out of them but found they were bound together. He started breathing faster, nostrils flaring in the dark.

He was as a newborn cast out into the vacuum of space.

He could feel his heart beat faster as his mind raced to keep up with this discovery of himself. Michael could feel his nerves begin to fire in all his limbs as electric panic coursed through his body. He lifted his head again and hit the boards, not four inches above him.

And again.

Banging his head against the darkness with the dirt washing his face.

He tugged at his arms. They were bound at the wrist and the

tape dug into him with each movement. His feet were fastened together at the ankles as he tried to kick at the darkness. His knees found the roof of his coffin as well and sent a spark of pain up his thighs. The motion caused more dirt to fall into his open eyes. He felt as if they were thoroughly crusted with grime.

Michael tried to force breath out of his mouth, but the tape's seal held. He felt as if his nostrils were too small to supply the air he needed as he kicked around in his confined cell. He could feel the sweat start to form on his body as he lurched back and forth.

Suddenly, he stilled. His mind slowly started to calm, moving from the rapid chaos of panic to the quiet, disembodied trance of a hopeless man.

Breathe, he thought.

Just breathe.

The sound of his lungs echoed in his head as he worked to slow himself down, his breathing easing to long, deliberate exhales. He closed his eyes to shut out the blackness and felt the sandpaper eyelids grind his retinas with fire.

Just breathe.

Michael could feel his pulse dissipate from the thunderous bass drum to a softer beat. His mind began to clear and assess his situation. Flailing around was not an option. If he wanted it all to end, as he had sometimes in life wished it would, then he could just go on doing what he was doing until the air ran out or the sand from above buried him in an hourglass of his own making. But his thoughts focused on hope, as they always seemed to. And so he willed his body to soften, to cooperate with his mind.

He focused on his hands. One by one he touched fingertip to fingertip, thumb to thumb, index to index, until he was assured they were all there. They were. For some reason this brought him a sense of comfort.

He tried to bring his hands to his face and failed several times. The box he was in wouldn't allow him to move his elbows from his sides, and when he kept them tucked in, his hands would press against the ceiling before he could bring them up to his chest.

Breathe.

Slowly and methodically he started to rotate his wrists back and forth, attempting to loosen the binding. It felt like duct tape. It was impossible for him to guess how many times it might have been wrapped around his wrists. He concentrated on his breathing and the rhythmic turns of his hands.

Inhale, twist; exhale, twist.

The hairs on his arm pulled with each turn until Michael was sure there were none left. He told himself he had all the time in the world, or at the least, all the time he had left, to get his hands free.

He kept twisting his wrists until the skin burned. In the dark he felt as if it had rubbed down to the bone. The dirt dripping from above him got under the tape, and though it worked as an antidote to the adhesive, it also added to the grinding down of flesh he felt with each twist.

Eventually he loosened the tape enough to turn his hands and grab onto each wrist. The tape had rolled in spots, and he could feel the stickiness of it mixed with warm fluid. It felt like raw skin and blood. In this position, and keeping his elbows in, he was able to force his hands up to his face where he instantly grabbed the strip across his mouth and pulled it free.

Like a skin diver resurfacing from a long dive, Michael gulped in the stale moldy air around him with an open mouth. The dirty and confined area flooded his senses, but he did not care at the moment. With his mouth free, he bit into the binding at his wrists, yanking and pulling with his teeth at tape and skin. His hands came free with ripping fire and he screamed.

Now unbound, Michael was able to feel around his confinement. He was, as he figured, in a box. He could feel the rough-hewn pine all around him. The cheapness of the wood and the fact that it was still holding up meant that he was not buried too deep. He assumed that too much earth would have come crashing in already. True or not, it added weight to a sliver of hope.

Michael had never been buried alive, but his mind offered up the blueprint of escape as if it had been programmed with the script for survival. Up. Up was the way to freedom. Scratch, claw upward. He had to get to the surface quickly—that or he would suffocate or be crushed before he knew it.

In the dark, he beat against the boards until his hands shot white-hot pains up his forearms. The dirt dropped onto his face as one of the boards cracked, filling his mouth and absorbing the air from his lungs. He spewed out the earth as he beat and dug and scraped upward.

The ground came down heavy around him like the pillars of Samson. His fingers gripped the soil and pulled.

He was a rhythmic engine of adrenaline, pushing up against the world and then shoving the incoming dirt down to the end of the box. Over and over again until the lid started to give more and more.

As the dirt flowed in, Michael worked to push it to the corners of the box. It was damp and clumpy but not tightly packed, two things incredibly in his favor. He worked furiously, his muscles screaming. His pulse pounding in his ears, stifled by the packed ground.

Then he felt it. His hand punched through to the cool air of the living world. With one last colossal effort, he got his feet under him and drove up through the loosening soil, breaking out to his waist into the majestic air of night.

Michael pulled himself out of the grave.

His whole body screamed for oxygen and the open air embraced his constricted muscles like a soothing nothingness. He lay on the ground and looked skyward, but his scratched and swollen eyes were packed in a gritty embalmer's salve, obscuring his vision into a watery blur. His breath formed small wisps of vapor in the dark and then dissipated.

He was in a forest. He dragged himself away from the entrance of his grave and braced himself against a tree. This was the closest to death that he had ever been, but he knew this was just the beginning. It would not end here. They would not let this rest. They would never let it rest until he was buried for good.

Michael ripped the last of the tape from his ankles and staggered to his feet. The smell of earth and mold permeated his senses as the chill of early autumn passed through him like a phantom breeze. The moon was out tonight, and it illuminated the woods with a menace, a black-and-white world on the verge of preparing itself to sleep through the upcoming winter, itself to be buried by the cold indifference of Mother Nature.

His eyes burned with the scratched rubbing of his lids still caked with dirt as he peered into the darkness. It was impossible to get his bearings. A blind man in a maze. All he could smell was the grave. But he listened to the quiet of the woods. Faintly he could hear running water in the distance. He took a step toward the sound, using the tree as a crutch and holding out one arm to break a fall that was all but assured. The noise of his own steps masked the water. He took a step, listened, took another.

Step.

Quiet.

Listen.

Repeat.

His body was wrecked. The men who had jumped him had pushed chemicals into his cells and then tenderized the muscles. He could feel the bruises on his back and chest rub against his clothing with each movement. His legs throbbed as if the sinews were wrapped too tightly around the bone. His hands were numb from the tape that had cut off his circulation. One finger felt dislocated, an issue that, with a tug and a shriek of agony, he quickly remedied.

Each step was a torturous effort, a willing of the mind to force the body forward.

Step.

Quiet.

Listen.

Repeat.

Soon the river could be heard consistently, and he stumbled forward with arms outstretched, knocking branches out of his way, tripping on exposed roots that lay hidden underfoot. Michael felt his way down the bank but soon lost all sense of up and down, and fell. He rolled down the embankment, adding bruises to his already beaten body, until he came to rest on the rocks next to the river. He got to his hands and knees and crawled to the water.

His throat was bone dry and the cool water shocked his system. The burning thirst overcame the repugnant smell of the river, and after a few gulps, he took a deep breath and plunged his face into the depths.

The coldness of the creek stung his senses, but he held himself under, flushing the earth from his eyes. The sensation of no pain in his sockets brought him back to the surface and he collapsed.

With his blurred vision slightly improved, his head resting on stone and sand, Michael peered out across the river, the moonlight slashing a gouge in the black water.

A puzzle piece locked into place in his brain, a sense of reassurance that he was closer to knowing where on earth he was. There was only one major river near Coldwater, a river named after the town or vice versa, and Michael knew this must be it. Coldwater River. From what he could tell, however, it was a portion that he was not familiar with.

He hadn't ventured out to the river much in his life anyway, but he knew enough to get some sense of direction. He was on the northern bank, judging from the slow current. The river cut against the upper part of the county and eventually made its way down south through Southwick, a good sixty miles away by road. Upriver, its source was hidden in the reptilian ridges of the north woods. He knew of several crossings, all of which would keep him away from Coldwater, but he wasn't quite sure which one he would come to first. Upriver would be the right course to take. He knew that, and it settled in his mind as the only correct option.

But for now his exhaustion was getting the best of him.

He crawled back to the embankment and found a hollow that fit his body decently enough. The night was cool but not frigid, and as he closed his eyes and listened to the flow of the river, he slept the sleep of a dead man, a dead man resurrected to a dark night.

The two men drove out from Coldwater that morning in silence, like the quiet of two men going to work, content to allow each other to wake up and process the morning without the aggravation of conversation. The truck motored north up the county road several miles and then headed east on gravel, and soon the gravel turned to dirt, and the dirt slowly gave way to a two-track heading into the woods. A developer had attempted to plot out a subdivision in the area but gave up when the market told him that folks from the city didn't want to live this far in the sticks.

Coldwater was sixty miles from the nearest "metropolis." City really. Sixty miles from where a family could buy groceries was the more proper way to say it.

The old Ford pushed on through the woods until the two-track finally gave up its ghost and terminated in a large clearing. The truck came to a stop. The passenger, who was half slumped in the seat, spoke first.

"Go on, Kyle, check it out so we can get out of here."

"Why me?"

"Well, I sure ain't going to do it!"

"Why don't we both go?"

"Come on. You know I got this bum leg in the mornings. Just walk up there, check it out, and we can head back."

Kyle hesitated in the driver seat. He stared into the woods. A tremor of fear slowly crept into his face as he white-knuckled the steering wheel.

"Here, take this," said James from the passenger seat, handing over a long hunting knife.

"What good is that going to do?"

"You serious? He's tied up . . . underground. How much more protection you need?"

Kyle stepped out of the truck, forcing his body to move as his nerves were getting the best of him. He almost tripped over one of the ruts in the mud made from the vehicles the night before. They were all over the clearing. He had been braver the night before, when there were so many of them, but now, on his own, his courage was nowhere to be found.

Kyle stood by the truck.

"Get going!" James yelled from the cab. "You're the one that wanted to come here. Now go check it out."

"Now that we're here . . . I don't know."

"Just do it! Otherwise you'll be bugging me all day to drive back out here. Go check it out, see that he's still buried, so we can go home."

"This is stupid."

"It is stupid, but you ain't going to leave me alone until you see it with your own eyes."

Kyle wiped a sweaty hand on his jeans. "I didn't sleep at all last night."

"I knew Haywood never should have let you come along."

"What does that mean?"

"It means exactly what I said. You were all gung ho yesterday, but now you're giving me an anxiety attack. Don't make me get out of this truck and drag you up there. 'Cause when you see he's still underground, I'll be mad at you for wasting my time."

"Okay, okay . . . calm down."

"Just go already."

Kyle closed the truck door and walked up the trail into the woods. About a quarter mile up, he saw the small clearing in the trees, saw the disturbed dirt. He inched his way closer, slowly. The sight scared him. He was startled by sounds coming from every side of him. The birds, the insects, the sound of the swaying trees in the light wind. He approached the clearing.

He saw the spot where they had buried Michael. Saw the earth pushed aside and sunk down into the crater, saw the drag marks from the hole and the footprints that led off deeper into the woods. In one quick second, his mind had processed the whole scene. His nightmare had come true, his guilt had been telling him all night that his fear was real.

Kyle turned and ran as if his life depended on it. He would have screamed, but his voice was lost, lost in the chaos. He could see the truck through the leaves. He ran, harder and harder, until he made the clearing. Jumping in the truck, he slammed it into drive, spun it around, and floored it back to the county road. James was almost ejected from his seat.

"What are you doing?" James shouted.

Kyle was silent. He felt as if his blood had stopped coursing through his veins. A cold sweat dripped from his hairline. His hands on the wheel shook uncontrollably as they guided the car rocketing through the woods.

"Kyle . . . Kyle!"

Kyle looked over at James. And with a whispered breath said, "He got out!"

ACKNOWLEDGMENTS

Many thanks to Andrea, who brought this story to light after being shelved for so many years. To the most incredible editor, Barb, thank you for taking the story to new levels with your attention to detail and precision. To Michele, Hannah, and Karen, thanks for putting up with me and getting the book into as many people's hands as possible.

To all my friends involved in the world of books: it would take pages upon pages to name you all. Thank you so much for your encouragement, interest, and humor. To the crew at the original H2, thanks for the inspiration.

And last, to Liz. You have let me believe in dreams that seem impossible, while keeping me rooted to the ground. I can never thank you enough.

Samuel Parker was born in the Michigan boondocks but was raised on a never-ending road trip through the US. Besides writing, he is a process junkie and the ex-guitarist for several metal bands you've never heard of. He lives in West Michigan with his wife and twin sons.

MEET SAMUEL PARKER

SAMUELPARKERBOOKS.COM

CPSIA information can be obtained
at www.ICGtesting.com
Printed in the USA
LVOW08*0924080117

520181LV00008B/57/P